Dare to Love

Iron Rogue 1

I0619841

Erotic Romance

Sandy Sullivan

Erotic Romance

Dare to Love – Iron Rogue 1
Copyright © 2018 Sandy Sullivan
Print Book ISBN: 978-1-944122-43-0

First E-book Publication: July 2018

Cover design by Dawne Dominique
Edited by Ariana Gaynor
Proofread by Maranda Raven
All cover art and logo copyright © 2018 by Sandy Sullivan

Dedication

To the rock and roller in all of us!
Enjoy!

DARE TO LOVE
Iron Rogue 1

Sandy Sullivan
Copyright © 2018

Chapter One

The deep *thrum* of the first chord rattled along his nerve endings. Goose bumps rose on his skin as his signature grin tilted his lips. God, he loved this song.

Smoke curled and floated along the stage, almost obliterating the floor from view. Inky blackness surrounded them, all except for a few lights near the edge of the stage for the effect. Camera flashes flickered in the crowd, exploding in a rapid burst of light so blinding he could barely see anything.

The throng went wild, screaming at the top of their lungs, chanting the title of their first song to hit the charts. *Dare to Love. Dare to Love. Dare to Love.* Hands in the air, lighters flickering in almost every palm, he'd been born for this.

Noah King watched from the side of the stage for a moment as his bandmates ramped up the crowd into a frenzy of screaming fans.

His heart thumped in his chest, his palms felt clammy, and his tongue was so dry it stuck to the roof of his mouth. Nerves always got him at the first riff of music, but the minute he stepped up to the mic, everything melted away except the music. He lived for it, breathed it, and loved it more than anything in his life.

He tipped the whiskey bottle to his lips for a moment, feeling the burn of the alcohol as it traveled down his throat. His stomach lurched for a second. *Damn it.* Nausea would play hell with him tonight.

Willing the sensation away, he grabbed the mic from the stagehand lurking in the shadows and made his way out to the front of the stage.

Darkness kept him from being seen until he counted to thirty and the lighting engineer would slowly bring them up and reveal the guys on the stage, outlining each of them until the spotlight hit them.

They'd done this thousands of times. Every night for so long, he couldn't remember what his bed at home felt like, much less the pleasure of fixing a meal in his kitchen or being able to wander through the rooms touching pictures of his family. There were times he hated the life he'd put together.

Tonight, he wasn't so sure.

The second riff of *Dare to Love* came from his lead guitarist, Alex, bringing the crowd to their feet as the lights slowly came up behind the band, throwing them into shadows.

He could see everything and everyone from his position at the edge of the platform. Women of every shape, size, ethnicity, and varying lack of clothing lined the rail. He let his gaze roam over each one, wondering how many of them would be waiting when they left the venue for the night. They never lacked for female company after a show. Booze, drugs, women, and fun. The life of a rock star.

His gaze rolled to the very edge of the stage on his right, locking on a women standing by herself near one of the security guards. She wasn't the typical groupie, not this one. Her body screamed something more, something enticing, something intriguing. Her long blonde hair lay in waves around her shoulders, the lights highlighting a shimmer of red. Long lashes framed clear green eyes that tilted at the outer corners and studied him from the top of his head to the tips of his boots. She wore a tight black V-neck t-shirt with *Rock Band News* written across her chest, emphasizing her gorgeous round breasts pressing against the front. Hip-hugging jeans encased legs that went on forever, a perfect outline to show every curve she owned, and black boots with spike heels wrapped around her ankles giving her that much more height. Red lips parted as she tilted her head a little to the left, a flirty smile on her mouth, making him wonder if she might be up for a little fun. *Stunning.*

And totally off limits.

Disappointment rushed down his spine even as his cock stood hard and ready. *Fucking hell.* It had been too damned long since he'd been that attracted to one woman, and he couldn't have her. He didn't have time for even a quick fuck, much to his dismay.

His attention shifted back to the fans as he belted out the first few words of the song, clear, deep, and right on target, the rest was a piece of cake. Money wasn't the reason he'd given up everything to be here. This was. The fans. For them, he'd do anything.

After tonight, it would be over. For a little while, anyway. They were taking a break he needed desperately.

His family needed him home.

The phone call he'd received two weeks ago had changed the course of the immediate future for the entire band. Their rescheduled shows would begin in a few months. Maybe by then, things would be settled. He wouldn't know until he had a chance to find out what was wrong at home.

First, he had to get through tonight which meant singing his heart out until he couldn't talk, doing the interview right after the show, and then hopping on the plane back to Iowa. He'd be home by morning.

As the band went through their entire set, Noah kept up the persona of the brooding rock star. The women threw themselves at them all, him, Alex, Aiden, and Dylan. None of them had a steady woman in their lives, but they didn't lack for female companionship after each show. It came with the territory. They collected more lingerie during a show than Victoria Secret's had in their showroom. Bra's, panties, negligee's, shirts, skirts, and bikini's seemed to appear from thin air. Sometimes the owner would find her way into their beds, but most of the time, they had no idea who the shit belonged to.

When the lights went down after the last set, he released a big sigh of relief. Done for now, thank goodness.

The crowd made their way out of the arena in droves, many waiting outside for the band to emerge for autographs. They'd do a few before they got on the plane. They couldn't disappoint their fans.

As they made their way to the dressing room, several people lined the hallway, slapping them on the back when they passed. Some were sponsors, some were groupies, and some were the guys who took care of their equipment. The concrete walls seemed sterile and uninviting, but it didn't matter. Backstage didn't need to be fancy, only the stage did to give the fans the show they paid for.

A large green door with Iron Rogue on it, indicating their private area for the night, stood to the right. Food of every kind lay spread out like a smorgasbord. Every band member could specify his favorite food and drink and it would appear, no questions asked. Several brands of alcohol were at their fingertips, liquor, wine, whiskey, or whatever. As the hottest band on the rock scene, they could have anything they wanted.

Tonight, it all seemed so hollow as Noah faced an impending shit-storm at home. He had no idea what awaited him when they got there, and his gut rolled with the thought.

Alex slapped him on the back as he grabbed a bottle of Grey Goose sitting on the table, sloshing a bit into a glass. "Great show."

"Yeah." Noah took a swig from the whiskey bottle sitting on the table. Everyone knew his penchant for Jack Daniel's and it was always available. *I really need to lay off this shit.*

Aiden took a seat on the couch, his big clunky black boots making a thud on the coffee table when he propped his feet up and leaned back with his hands across his abdomen. "Damn, I'm glad for this break."

"You and me both, brother," Dylan replied, wrapping his arm around a busty brunette who had somehow made it past the security guard at the door.

Noah frowned at the girl, tipping his head to indicate she needed to leave.

"What?" Dylan grabbed her left breast with his palm. "She's for later."

Pointing the whiskey bottle at the door, Noah didn't give Dylan a choice. The girl had to go. "We need to do this interview so I can get the hell out of here to the airport. We don't have time for chicks tonight unless it's once we make it home."

"Fuck. Fine." Dylan brought her to her feet as escorted her to the door. "I'll catch you later, sweetheart."

She glanced over Dylan's shoulder and caught Noah's gaze. He knew her type. Lay a rock star and she'd be gone by morning with her story and a pair of torn panties to show to her friends.

Rick came through the door as she was leaving. "Okay. The reporter will be here in a moment. Her name is Victoria Richmond with Rock Band News. You guys be nice. We need this interview so we can keep you in the papers until you are back on the road in a few months."

A soft knock sounded on the door, giving away her presence. Rick pulled it open, blocking the visitor from their sight for a moment as he spoke softly to her. When he stepped back, Noah's breath caught. It was the blonde from the side of the stage, every glorious inch of her standing right in front of him.

"Guys, this is Victoria."

"Tori, please." She did a little finger wave as she moved a little closer.

Her gaze ricocheted from one guy to the next until it landed on him. His breath left in a soft whoosh as his stomach knotted for a second. He brought the bottle of Jack to his lips and took another long swallow. Heat simmered along his nerves, making him feel hot all over. The need to touch her rushed his system. He wanted to run his hands over her curves, feel her mold to his chest and sigh in delight as he brought their mouths together in a desperate kiss. *God, I need to get laid.*

"Relax gentleman. I'm not here to grill you. We'll make this short and sweet so you can get on your way. I know you have a lot to do." She took a chair in the corner, turning it so she faced them all. "I have a few questions for each of you, so we'll start with that."

Noah couldn't keep his eyes off her. Women weren't new to him. He'd been with his share that came with their lifestyle, and at thirty plus, he certainly knew his way around a woman's body. Hers was something he would love to roam with his hands, his mouth, and his tongue.

When her gaze shot to him, he knew it was his turn.

"Noah, right?" she asked, her gorgeous eyes fixed on his face as they narrowed slightly with concentration.

"Yeah."

"All right, Noah. Tell me about growing up in Iowa. I know a little about your background, but not a lot. Did you live on a farm?"

A small chuckle left his mouth as he tipped the whiskey bottle to his lips again. If you could call the patch of ground his dad worked a farm. "Sure did. Corn and everything."

The scratching of her pen across the paper came to him over the din of the music being piped into the room. "How did you start the band?"

Noah glanced at all the guys before coming back to her. They meant the world to him even if they were a pain in the ass most of the time. He wouldn't be where he was without them and he knew it. They had his back just as he had theirs. "All of us knew each other in high school. I sang in the school choir and met Alex there. He already played guitar, so we decided to start up a garage band. He knew Dylan and Aiden from the next town over since Dylan had dated his sister. Once we all got together, it came together pretty easily."

"You became very popular a few years ago, from what I've read." She jotted something on her notebook before catching his eye again. Curiosity and something intense reflected back, something he felt a huge need to explore. "Dare to Love was your first major hit, right?"

"Yes it was."

"You wrote it?"

"Yes. Me and Alex."

She tucked a stray piece of hair behind her ear, the strand looking soft and silky to the touch. He itched with the desire to rub it between his fingers. Whiskey burned down his throat as he took another long swallow.

"Alex, did this song have a specific meaning to it? I mean the lyrics are very potent and have a lot of heart to them."

"You'll have to ask Noah that one. He wrote the lyrics. I wrote the music." Alex leaned back in the chair, resting his hands over his abdomen and lacing his fingers together.

Her gaze moved back to him, and panic set in. His stomach clenched, nausea curling in his gut. His throat went dry as he tried to push the foolish wishes of a teenage boy to the pit of his heart. He didn't want to talk about it with anyone, much less a reporter. Even the guys didn't know the depth of those lyrics. "That's personal."

Her perfectly arched eyebrows pulled down in the center as a frown settled on her lips. "I'm sorry, but your fans want to know. Lyrics to any song are usually very personal and tell a story of something the artist went through."

The tapping of her pen on the notebook pissed him off. Everything about her pissed him off from her kissable mouth to the long hair he wanted to wrap his fist in while he threaded his cock between her pouty lips. *Off limits. Off limits.* Those perky breasts pushing against her Rock Band News t-shirt had him curling his hands into fists to keep from reaching for her. That curvy waist meant for a man's hands to hold her steady while he fucked her from behind, and her long legs perfect for wrapping around a man's hips.

God damn it!

Inhaling sharply, he focused back on something besides fucking her. She didn't need to know what those lyrics meant, only he did, no one else. He jumped to his feet, grabbed the bottle of Jack and took a long pull before he leveled his gaze on her again. "This interview is over. Rick, get her out of here."

"But—"

"But nothing." He swallowed several gulps of the whiskey, hoping they would numb him. Numb was good. He ran his hand through his hair, restlessness gripped him like a fist. He needed to get out of there. His footsteps took him back and forth across the expanse of the room. "I said, get her out of here! Now!"

After a moment of silence, she picked up her bag from the floor and turned to look at him again. "I'm sorry if I hit a nerve, but I am a reporter and it's my job to get the story your fans want to read." She glanced at all of them for a moment. "Thank you, gentlemen, for the interview. I hope the rest of your tour this year is a major success, and I hope to catch you later on."

He felt her gaze on him for a moment as he moved toward the adjoining door where their personal items were and stopped with his hand on the doorknob. Interviews sucked, and this one had been no different. It didn't matter that Tori was gorgeous and had a body he would love to see naked beneath him. Complications like her, he didn't need.

When the outer door closed, he breathed a sigh of relief before Rick went off.

Rick grabbed his shoulder, spinning him back around to face the group. "What the hell, Noah. I told you what this article meant for you guys while you're going to be off the tour for a few months so you can deal with whatever personal shit you have going on at home."

Rage settled in his gut. Rick worked for him, for them. If he didn't like the way Noah handled himself, then he could go to hell and take everyone else with him. "I don't give a fuck. I won't discuss that song with anyone, not her, not you, not anyone, so back the hell off." He slammed the door in Rick's face and then proceeded to bang his head against the panel for a moment. She'd hit too close to home with that one and he wasn't in any mood to deal with a nosy reporter, rosy lips or not.

His plane awaited and so did the drama at home. He needed a break.

* * * *

The arrogant, stubborn, fucking gorgeous lead singer of Iron Rogue had his manager shove her out, slamming the door in her face. *Damn him!* A crowd of a hundred people or more hung out near the doors, waiting. Tori stood nearby with her bag in hand as she tried to calm her racing pulse by pacing back and forth. It didn't help one bit. Mostly even-tempered, she didn't lose her cool often, but Noah had shredded her control and then some.

It had taken six months of finagling to get her boss to let her do the interview of the band and she blew it. She had Noah King right where she wanted him, on the verge of telling her what everyone in the rock world wanted to know. Why were the lyrics for Dare to Love such a secret as to their meaning? Why did it upset him so much too even talk about that song? It seemed even the other guys in the band didn't know, and that intrigued her even more.

Not that he was a chore to look at. His dark hair hung well past his shoulders in typical rock star fashion, dark eyes that reminded her of melted chocolate with flecks of almonds in them, a closely cropped beard framed his mouth and along his jawline, broad shoulders, sculpted pecs, strong and capable biceps, tapered waist, abs ripped enough to want to lick something off of, and thighs solid enough to bounce quarters from. He was the total package and some change, but he was also moody, arrogant, demanding, and from what everyone knew, had an alcohol problem.

The way he'd looked at her, like he wanted to undress her and devour her, had her thinking he might tell her. In the next second, he'd shut down, totally turned off every emotion gleaming in his eyes, and kicked her out of the room. She'd hit a nerve, that's for sure. Something wasn't right and by God, she planned to find out what it was.

The door to the venue banged open, slamming against the wall, and the band strode out in a flurry of screaming fans. Watching for a moment, she could see how the guys worked the crowd, pausing to sign a few autographs and take a picture with a fan. The women drooled and the men hanging around seemed in awe. No wonder they sold millions of albums. Their fans loved them.

The crowd parted slightly outside the ropes and behind the security guards as they made their way toward a long black car waiting to the right, stopping every few feet to greet another fan.

Several roadies rolled out the equipment boxes into the waiting trucks behind them, never even noticing the wild scene going on around them. They had a job to do, and they did it well from what she could see.

Desperate times called for desperate measures. She had to get her story one way or another. One crazy thought raced through her head as she tried to come up with a plan. *This is crazy. I can't do this.* Biting her thumbnail, she rolled the idea around in her head over and over until she came to the same conclusion. She wasn't giving up this chance for anything in the world. Her career depended on it.

Taking a deep breath, she skirted around the back side of the limo, noticing the trunk open but all the guys' suitcases were already in there. Sending up a little prayer, she jumped inside and pulled it closed behind her. If they found her, they'd kill her probably, and then throw her body somewhere along the road. She had no idea where they were going, but everything in her life rode on this.

Within a few moments, the guy's voices got louder as they climbed inside the car, the door shut, and they were moving.

Holy crap!

Darkness surrounded her. She couldn't see her hand in front of her face. Her cell phone dug into her hip where she lay on her side, cramping the muscle into a Charlie horse. Clutching her bag to her chest, she prayed they'd get to their destination quickly. Claustrophobia wasn't anything to laugh at, and she only had a mild case, enough to make her breathing choppy and her pulse race. *I'll be okay. It's only for a little bit. We'll stop and I'll figure out the next step in this crazy plan.*

They continued along for several miles even though she couldn't tell where they were headed. Cars honked nearby as they raced past them, engines roared, and people screamed out their windows. The tires of the car rode over the rumble strips. God, she hated that. It was one of her biggest pet peeves, annoying her beyond comprehension until it stopped and she could breathe again. Sweat dotted her temples and her upper lip. Nausea gripped her stomach, making that pizza she had before the concert iffy at best. She wished she had some water, although that would probably come back up if she drank any. *Breathe, just breathe.*

Quiet descended except for distant rumblings, a noise she couldn't place. She could hear the guys laughing in the car, but the words were incomprehensible. This hell had to be over soon, she hoped.

When the car finally stopped and the trunk lid popped open, she scrambled out and slipped under the bottom of the car, hoping no one had seen her. She held her breath, afraid they might be able to hear the rasping sound as it escaped her lips. The long red carpet leading from where the car stopped to the plane gave her some relief for the hot pavement under her while she waited. Her hair stuck to her neck, making it itch with irritation as she debated her sanity. *This is nuts. I'm nuts for even trying this.*

Peering from under the car, she could see what appeared to be a large private jet sitting not one hundred yards away with the back door open as a catering service loaded it. *A plane? They own a fucking plane?*

Flying wasn't one of her favorite things to do. Airsickness usually played hell with her when she did, but come hell or high water, she was going to get the story.

Asphalt dug into her elbows when she scooted toward the side away from the plane, crouched against the passenger door of the car, before moving around the front. Sitting back on haunches, she looked around the front fender. Loud, angry voices reached her on the wind.

Tori could see the four guys and the manager standing near the bottom of the stairs to the plane as they argued. Noah stood with his hands on his hips, his hair blowing around his face in a dark cloud, matching the thundering expression in his eyes. To say he was pissed was the understatement of the century. "I don't care, Rick. She was digging where she shouldn't be. It is none of her business where those lyrics came from."

"It's only an article, Noah. She didn't want your personal shit to drag through the mud." Rick stood toe to toe with Noah, although Noah's height had him by a good six inches. Their manager wasn't a big man, other than his paunch hanging over the waistband of his pants. His eyes narrowed as they focused on Noah, and she could see the indignation Noah wore like a shield. Rick was their manager and their friend, she'd thought. He'd been with them a long time, but it sounded as if Noah wasn't going to give an inch.

"It would have been."

"I don't get it. It was your first big hit. People want to know."

"Too fucking bad."

Rick waved his hand in front of his face, his large diamond studded ring reflecting the lights from the nearby building. He obviously made good money working for Iron Rogue if she was any judge of flashy jewelry. "It doesn't matter now anyway, Noah. You've ruined the article. She'll print what she wants and that will be that. Who knows, she may just make something up."

"The hell she will. I'll have her and the magazine in court so fast, her head will spin like she's possessed."

Their voices faded a bit as Tori scooted around the back of the truck parked near the plane and just as the driver got into the cab, she hurried up the stairs. A door near the back looked like a safe place to hide, something compact and discreet. When she pulled it open, she almost giggled. It was the bathroom, luxury and all with its gold gilded mirror, large marble sink in the corner, and holy hell, it even had a full shower. She'd hide here until she decided the next step in her plan.

Within seconds she heard the guys scramble aboard the plane, the door shut, and the engines start. She hoped this wasn't a long flight. Flying made her nervous.

Her stomach dropped the moment the wheels came off the ground and she sank to the floor of the compact bathroom as her throat began to burn and her eyes watered. *I won't be sick. I won't be sick. I won't be sick.*

"Oh shit," she whispered, breathing through her nose as she tried desperately not to puke.

At least she was in the bathroom.

She rolled to her knees, flipped open the lid on the toilet, and threw up everything in her stomach. *Pepperoni doesn't come back up well.*

Several dry heaves later, she laid her head against the cool seat hoping she wouldn't throw up again.

The door flew open, crashing against the side of the hallway, banging so loud she thought for sure it had left a hole in the very expensive wall.

"What the fuck?"

After a deep breath through her nose, she wiped her mouth with the back of her hand and slowly turned around, her butt landing on the floor with a thump.

Noah stood in the doorway, his dark hair pushed back off his forehead and his brown eyes narrowed and very, very angry. "How the hell did you get in here?"

Her mouth opened, but nothing came out as her stomach rolled again, and she spun around to throw up in the toilet. The groan that left her lips was desperate and sickly. A soft tug on her hair kept it back off her face, while she braced her palms on the seat. The moment she finished, she laid her cheek against the toilet seat and gulped a few breaths of air, hoping to settle the rolling.

"Shit." He disappeared a moment before he came back with a wet, cold washcloth in his hand. "Here."

"I'm sorry," she whispered, wiping the wonderful coldness against her cheeks.

"Let me help you." He pulled her to her feet, wrapped an arm around her waist before settling her on one of the leather seats.

He came back a moment later with a glass of something bubbly in some ice. "Ginger Ale. Sip it. It will help settle your stomach. Do you get motion sick all the time?"

She nodded, afraid to answer until she was able to sip the icy liquid. Her eyes teared up when she glanced up and caught him staring at her, his eyes hooded and unreadable, his lips slashed in a straight line across his gorgeous mouth, and his hands fisted at his sides.

He flopped down in the seat across from her, crossing his booted feet at the ankles and laying his folded fingers over his taut stomach.

Terrified she'd made a huge mistake, she started to try to explain, but first, she needed to know one thing. "Where are we going?"

One eyebrow lifted over his left eye. "You stowed away on our private plane and you don't even know where we're headed?"

She shook her head, hoping it wouldn't cause her nausea to return. *So far, so good.*

He studied her for a moment as if he was trying to decide whether to trust her with their destination. "We are going home, to Iowa."

"Your break from the tour includes going home? I would have thought you might go somewhere exotic, like Hawaii or Jamaica."

"If you must know, yes. Home it is this time."

He wasn't giving her much information. Then again, why would he? She had invaded his privacy and the privacy of his bandmates. He could have her arrested the minute they touched down and ruin her career in the process.

This whole thing was a really bad idea.

"Why are you here?" he asked, his gaze sliding over her hair and face.

Hoping the truth was better than any lie she could come up with, she said, "I thought if I had a chance to explain things a little better about the questions back there, I might be able to convince you I'm sincere in my need to know."

His eyes narrowed and became unreadable again as the angry Noah returned. "In other words, you want to dig further."

Her shoulders lifted in a shrug. "Well, yes, I guess so, but it's for your fans, Noah."

His lips thinned out, drawing her gaze to the annoyed look on his face and then to the irritated tapping of his fingers resting on the arm of the chair. "That part of my life is not for my fans. It has nothing to do with them, so leave them out of it. Do you not understand privacy?"

"Hey, what's going on back here?" Alex slid to a stop at the doorway. "What's she doing here?"

"I'm trying to find out that very thing. Other than she stowed away, I haven't gotten much else."

"Sweet!" Alex's eyes glittered with a challenge. "At least we have some pretty company on the flight home." He took her hand, bringing her to her feet. "Come on out front. You can tell us about you since you know all about us."

Alex tucked her hand in the crook of his arm, leading her down the narrow walkway and into the front of the plane where the other guys in the band sat. Aiden had one of his guitars across his lap, picking out a tune she hadn't heard before as he wrote down some notes. He didn't seem to even notice she was there. Dylan had a set of earphones in as he listened to something on the phone in his hand without lifting his eyes. Alex put her in a chair across from him as he looked her up and down, his gaze giving an appreciative sweep of her body.

After he picked up his beer, Alex asked, "So beautiful lady. How did you manage to get on our plane?"

"I snuck up the back stairs after the caterers were done."

"And how did you get to the locked, private airport parking?" Noah took the seat next to her, trapping her next to him on the long, luxurious couch.

"I stowed away in the trunk of the limo."

"Clever girl. I will have to fire the limo driver and our security if it was that easy," Noah said, leaning back against the cushion behind him. "What is your plan once we get to Iowa?"

She glanced down at her hands before bringing her gaze back to the intense man next to her. "I don't know. I wanted to get to know you guys on a personal level, I guess, so I can convey the real you to your fans on that plain of existence. They would die for the personal touch to the article." *This was probably the worst idea I've ever come up with.* The seam on the inside of her thigh frayed a little as she picked at it with her fingernail before bringing her gaze back to his.

Noah's eyes narrowed, the brown becoming more of an amber color. Irritation came off him in waves, and she decided right then it wasn't a good idea to piss off the leader of Iron Rogue. He could probably squash her career with one phone call.

She glanced at Dylan and Aiden, both seemed preoccupied or just didn't care that she was there. Alex looked amused. "I'm really sorry. I guess I didn't think this through very well, but you didn't give me much choice, Noah. You shut me down the minute things got a little close to home."

Pinching the bridge of his nose with his finger and thumb, he locked those intense eyes on her. "There is a reason for that, Victoria. I don't want my private life out there for people to pick apart. I take my privacy very seriously and having you digging where your pretty nose doesn't belong makes me twitch."

Her full name coming from his lips sent shivers down her arms. She didn't care for her given name much, but having him say it did funny things to her insides. *I am not attracted to Noah King. He's egotistical, demanding, and a player from the letter p.* "I get that, I really do, but think of your fans. They adore you and inhale every tidbit about you guys that's printed. I'm trying to give them what they want."

He sat forward on the couch, dropping his hands between his parted knees as he speared her with his disgust. "What about what we want? Did you ever think of that? We are human beings with lives outside of the rock world. Hell, we can't piss without someone wanting to know what color it is."

Her lip became trapped between her teeth as she contemplated what he said. What would it be like to have every nuance of your existence splashed across the pages of a magazine, from the color of your underwear to who you went to dinner with the night before? She'd always kept her personal thoughts and feelings about her subjects out of the middle of whatever she was writing, but she didn't have to worry about someone following her home, or calling her on the phone if they got her number even though it was unlisted. She didn't have to dissect each relationship wondering if the person she liked was only after fame or her money.

Noah focused on her face as a smile lifted the corners of his lips. The grin was one of the things she'd always liked about him, but this one looked like it meant trouble with a capital T. Somehow, that smile didn't bode well for *her*.

"Since you are so hell-bent on learning about our personal lives, we are going to give you the chance. You'll stay with us, eat with us, go wherever we go, and you will learn all there is to know about us. At the end of our stint in Iowa, if you still think it is appropriate for our *fans* to know every little thing, then by all means, you write that article and include our most intimate details. If you realize when this is over that we are not everything you thought you knew, you will leave us in peace from now on."

Her stomach flipped over. *Learn everything about each one of the guys? This is the chance of a lifetime for me as a reporter, but can I really get that close to them and keep me in one piece?*

Chapter Two

The plane touched down with a *screech* as Tori clutched the arms of the couch. Her face was so pale her green eyes looked huge. Her comfort didn't matter one bit to him at the moment. *I don't give a shit whether she even has clean underwear.* He rubbed his index finger over the hair along his chin as he watched her. *She could go without underwear altogether. That would be fine with me.*

Flying didn't bother Noah a bit, he'd done it so many times. It helped having their own plane. They could come and go as they pleased from concerts and such without having to worry much about schedules. The luxury of having it was their one extravagant purchase when they'd hit it big. The inside had several leather captain's chairs or they could sit on the two couches lining either side of the plane.

She heaved a sigh of relief as the plane slowed and begun to taxi into a spot so they could unload.

Des Moines was a good-sized town at over two hundred thousand people, but there were a ton of smaller ones scattered within a couple of hours from the city. That was where they were headed, south about sixty miles to their hometown of Sommerton. It wasn't much to look at. They had two stop lights in the center of town that blinked yellow after ten at night when the whole town shut down and rolled up the sidewalks. Nothing was open except the local bar after seven anyway.

Noah couldn't wait to get home.

As they descended the stairs from the plane a black sedan pulled up beside them. There were no pretenses in Iowa for this famous rock band.

A young guy wearing a t-shirt, jeans, and a ball cap stepped out of the driver's side. "Noah! Hey, man, good to see you!"

"Ethan. Thanks for picking us up."

"No problem, man." He looked over at the others. "Alex. Aiden, Dylan. You all look great." His gaze hit on Tori. "Well, hello there. Who might you be?" Ethan asked, stepping forward and taking Tori's hand.

"Victoria Richmond, but you can call me Tori."

"Nice to meet you, Tori. How did you end up with these losers?"

She smiled, unable to keep from liking the guy in front of her, although she wasn't sure how he fit in with Iron Rogue. Her voice dropped to a loud whisper, "I stowed away on the plane."

His gaze shot to Noah, who answered with a nod. "She's a reporter for Rock Band News, we met at the last tour stop."

Ethan laughed so hard he had to let go of her hand and bend over at the waist. "Oh my God! That is priceless." He wiped his eyes as he continued to laugh. "The way you avoid the press at all cost, and here you are with one in your midst. What exactly are you going to do with her?"

"She's going to stay with us for the next few weeks. She is hell-bent on giving our fans a look into the life of a rock star, a personal look, so we are obliging her."

"Oh, this is good." Ethan smiled. "I'll be happy to show you around and give you my take on these pain in the asses."

"I'm sure that would be great."

He tucked her hand into the crook of his arm and led her to the car, leaving Noah and rest of them standing next to their bags. He glanced back at the others and shrugged as he grabbed his suitcase and hefted it into the trunk of the car.

"I hope there is somewhere to shop for clothes in town. I obviously didn't bring anything with me." She held up her tote bag. "This only has my computer, notebook, chargers, and wallet in it."

Noah frowned, realizing she indeed had nothing, no shampoo, brush, toothbrush, or anything to sleep in. This would be difficult. "There really isn't tonight. Everything in town will be locked up tight, and the road between here and there doesn't have much for retail. I'm sure we can find you something to sleep in, though."

The eyebrow over her right eye went up in a cocky little lift. "Exactly where *am* I going to sleep?"

"I have extra bedrooms at my house," he said, wishing he hadn't suggested this. The feeling of getting in way over his head weighed on him. He liked his privacy even if he was back home for the sake of his family. Guests weren't always a welcome thing at his house, but since this was his idea, he should be the one taking care of her.

A small smile played on her lips as her gaze met his. He could almost see the wheels turning in that pretty head of hers while she calculated how much information she would be able to glean while she stayed under his roof. *Damn it! This is going to be a clusterfuck.*

The guys all had their own places when they were in town. Alex had a pretty good size house on the outskirts of town to the north with a little land, a great pool for the summer heat, and an awesome backyard. Dylan had taken some of his money and built a cabin in the middle of a hundred acres of old growth trees and some farmland. He rented the land out to a local guy who did the farming, but Dylan had his place smack in the center so no one could see him when he was home. Then there was Aiden. He'd been born and raised in the next town over, but when he was young his dad had taken off, leaving his mother alone to raise him on her own. She still worked in town at a local restaurant waiting tables even though she didn't need to. Aiden lived with her when he was home, taking care of her house and yard. His part of the place was the basement that had a huge soundproofed apartment so he could play his guitar when he wanted and not disturb anyone.

Noah lived in an old two-story farmhouse on a chunk of property he'd purchased next to his parents. Farm life was nothing new to him although when he was growing up, he hated living on a farm. Work from sun up until sun down, feeding cattle, chickens, goats, and whatever else his dad thought might make some money. His dad still farmed the land.

These days he had his studio built onto the barn on his property, and he was refurbishing the old farmhouse a little at a time when he was home. The state-of-the-art studio seemed so out of place in the half run-down structure, but it was somewhere he could go and be alone to think, write lyrics, and contemplate what the hell he wanted out of his life. These days, he wasn't sure.

As he'd grown older, he'd come to cherish the peacefulness of living out in the country. No cars. No city noise. No crazy people. Just quiet.

"Let's get moving. It's getting late or should I say early since it's two in the morning, and I'd like to get a little shut-eye before we start dealing with shit here," Alex said, sliding into the back seat of the sedan.

Ethan was to drop them all off at their houses one at a time. The total trip would take probably an hour once they hit town. None of them lived very close together.

Since they hadn't planned on an extra person in the car, the seating arrangement left a lot to be desired. Tori was in the middle of the front seat, situated with her thigh pressed hard against Noah's. Damn if he didn't like the pressure of it there. *I should have sat in the back.* The scent of her perfume seemed to seep right into his veins and shoot straight to his balls.

Their driver chatted away with Tori all the way to town where once she saw the darkened streets and storefronts, she sighed.

"Something wrong?"

"I was hoping for something to eat. I haven't eaten since lunch yesterday."

"Sorry. There won't be anything open at this time of night, not even the local bars."

"No McD's or anything?"

"Nope." He shifted a little closer to the door, needing distance. Heat permeated where they touched, burning his skin like an open flame to the flesh. Need snaked along his nerves, making him aware of how long it had been since he'd been with a woman. *Too damn long.* "Once we get to my house, I should have something in the freezer you can warm up."

"That would be wonderful. Thank you, Noah."

His chest squeezed as he met her gaze. She had the prettiest eyes he'd ever seen and the most kissable mouth, but he didn't dare go there. Temporary women were what he was into, and using her for her short stint in town wasn't a good idea even if she was onboard with the plan. He was here to take care of some family business, nothing more. He cleared his throat and focused out the front windshield. Yellow lines in the center of the road whizzed past. The white line on his right stretched solid and straight into the night just beyond the headlights of the car. He should rest, sleep for a few minutes. The next few weeks were going to be hell, and he hadn't slept well in days.

Dylan, Alex, and Aiden talked in the back seat, discussing the performance they'd just come from. Noah knew they'd done well, they always did. Everything went off without a hitch from the lights to the sound and the crowd. The fans were fabulous.

"The crowd was really into it tonight," Alex said, tapping his fingers on his thigh. "I could feel the excitement all the way up on the stage."

Dylan played drums near the back of the setup and even though he was the quiet one of the bunch, he liked to give his opinion on their songs. "Yeah, but I think we should switch out the playlist next time. Dare to Love is our signature song. I don't think we should lead with it."

"Are you kidding, man?" Aiden played bass and definitely wasn't quiet. "We have to pump them up the minute we hit the stage, if we don't we'll lose them to the refreshment stand."

Tori's voice came at it from the side. "Do you want my opinion from a fan point of view?"

"No," Noah said, even though the guys in the back said yes very loudly.

"We need a new song. Hopefully, while we are on this little forced vacation, maybe Alex and Noah can come up with something." Dylan tapped Noah on the back of the head. "You got anything in there, Noah? We need some fresh stuff."

"From what I saw being in the audience for the show, the fans love your signature song. They really do, but Dylan is right. You need something new, first of all, and second, you need to hold that one to the end. They come to hear it. If they haven't heard it yet, they'll stay to hear it. It's the one they know the best."

Damn her smug look and pouty mouth that he wanted to kiss as badly as he needed his next breath. "We have two months. If I can, I'll come up with a new song. You know I haven't written anything in quite a while."

"You need to lay off the Jack, Noah. Maybe you can write better without it."

"None of your business, Alex." He didn't even look behind him.

"Yes, it is. You're my best friend. I don't want to see you go down that shit hole."

"I'm not."

"Is your stomach better? I mean, with all the nausea and pain you've been having, you probably need to see the doctor about it."

Noah glanced at Tori, reading the curiosity in her gaze. They didn't need to be airing this crap in front of her. The last thing she needed was more shit to print. "It's nothing, Alex. Lay off, man." His gaze met Tori's. "That is not to be printed. I will tell you what you can put in an article. Understood?"

"Sure, Noah."

"Good."

His breath released in a long, pent-up sigh. The last thing he needed was any of his health issues hitting the magazines, and he sure didn't need anyone speculating about a drinking problem he did or didn't have.

Several tense moments later, they pulled up to Alex's house. The trunk popped open as he climbed from the car.

"Call you tomorrow, Noah."

"Sure."

Alex disappeared inside his house, the lights flicking on in the front window for a moment as Ethan pulled back out onto the street. Next would be Aiden since he lived in town, and then they'd drop Dylan off. Noah would be last.

"I can move to the back, if you want."

"No, it's fine. We should be at Aiden's in a little bit, then I'll move back there."

Her hand rested on her thigh, her fingers curling underneath as if she was trying to keep them to herself. He knew the pulsating electricity rushing between them was bad. It would complicate so many things, although his skin tingled where they touched. All he'd have to do is put his arm behind her, and she would be able to lean into him. *Nope. Not going there.*

The soft, silky strands of her hair brushed his arm, leaving a tickling sensation along his skin. Blonde and long was his favorite and almost made him rock hard. He loved being able to bind his fist in a woman's hair.

Her scent wrapped itself around his senses, something tangy and sweet he couldn't place. His thoughts drifted to whether that same scent lingered in the crease of her thigh.

His cock hardened behind the leather of his pants, the zipper digging into his flesh like teeth. *Not such a good idea to go commando tonight.*

He shortened his breathing so he wouldn't brush against her arm, without much luck. The confines of the car and the fact that he wasn't a small man, made it that much more difficult to ignore the sensations she was causing.

A moment later they pulled into Aiden's place.

"Nice," she said, checking out the front of the house through the windshield.

"Thanks. I bought it a few years ago for my mom. My place is in the basement."

She giggled and the sound reverberated along his spine. Damn, it was cute.

"You live in your mother's basement?"

Aiden grinned. "Yep. It's soundproof."

"Smart."

"I thought so. I'll show it to you sometime while you're here."

"That would be great."

Aiden slipped out of the car, meeting Noah at the door. "Behave yourself, Noah."

"What the hell?"

"You'll have a beautiful woman under your roof at least for one night, dressed in nothing but one of your t-shirts. Keep your hands to yourself."

"I don't need her kind of distraction."

"Maybe, maybe not. Either way, man, control your baser instincts." Aiden smiled at Tori and waved as he stopped on the porch. "See you later."

Noah slid into the back seat, slamming the door as he let his frustrations get the best of him for a moment. What he'd said to Aiden was true. He didn't need to feel her petite body next to his, nor the way her breasts would mold to his chest and fit perfectly in his palms.

Ah hell. It's going to be a long and painful night at this rate.

* * * *

They pulled into Noah's driveway and when Tori got a good look at his house, she was shocked. It was a farmhouse with a large wrap around porch, pretty green shutters, and a green front door. She couldn't tell much more about it in the darkness with only the light over the barn to illuminate the yard, but she liked it, like it a lot.

"How pretty."

"Thanks," he said, pushing open the door and moving around the back to grab his bag with her on his heels. "It's not much. I'm renovating it."

"It's very homey."

"And private." His gaze locked on hers. "Remember, I value my privacy."

"I'm aware, Noah. I won't be going to Facebook and posting your address."

"I would hope not."

She followed him up the stairs as the lights of the sedan disappeared down the driveway. Noah unlocked the front door, flipped on the porch light, and moved inside to the entryway. A tall coat rack with a bench seat sat next to the wall. It reminded her of one of those pieces you saw on Wayfair.

Noah put his bag on the bench and headed down the hall, flipping on lights as he went.

A kitchen lay to her right with gorgeous white cabinets and a gold and brown veined granite countertop. There was a huge island in the center of the room with a white farmhouse sink and antique brass faucet. The island had three stools with cowhide seats under the edge. Dark stained wood floors gleamed in the light.

"This is gorgeous," she said, running her fingers along the island countertop.

"The kitchen was the first room I redid. I like to cook when I'm home so I wanted it done. The bedrooms aren't redone yet, nor is the living room and den space."

Curiosity won out. Even a little information from the reclusive leader of the band was better than nothing. "How long have you lived here?"

"About three years, but I'm not home a lot as you probably guessed." He stuffed his hands into the front pockets of his pants as he rocked back on his heels. "Follow me and I'll show you where you can sleep."

"Great. I'm pretty tired. It's been a long day."

Watching his gorgeous ass move up the stairs was torture enough, but encased in leather pants simply made her drool. As he went around the corner at the top of the stairs, she followed like a lost puppy wanting to be stroked by her master's hand. *This is ridiculous. He's just a guy.*

The light came on with a click as he stopped at a doorway. "You can sleep in here."

When she glanced inside the room, she was struck by the simplicity of the décor. The wrought iron bed screamed antique with its curving lines and small flowers at each juncture of connection. The white and red comforter looked warm and inviting. The walls were painted white with little adornment, and she could tell he hadn't really worked on this room, but it was still gorgeous. "It's beautiful, Noah. Thank you."

"There is a bathroom through there." He glanced at the floor and then back at her, his hair falling to the side of his face, making him look almost human. "Lock the door when you're in there. It connects to my room."

Heat flushed her cheeks as an image of him naked in the shower flashed across her mind. *Holy crap! I need to get myself under control. This is nuts.* "Uh, right. Lock the door."

"You can sleep as late as you'd like. We won't be doing much tomorrow since we got in so late tonight. I need to go to my parents' place tomorrow morning or should I say this morning. I might not be here when you wake up." He pulled his long hair back off his face and secured it with an elastic band she hadn't been aware he'd had wrapped around his wrist. "I'll have coffee made, if you drink it, and there is milk and cereal in the cupboard until I get to the store."

"I appreciate it. Thank you again. This is more than I could have expected due to the way I ended up here."

His gorgeous full lips lifted in a crooked grin. "We can discuss payment later." The air thickened around them, sizzling as if lightning were building within a storm. "I'll be back in a second with something for you to sleep in." He stepped back through the doorway and shut the door behind him.

Her breath escaped in a rush as she stuffed her hands into the front pockets of her jeans. "Wow."

Unsure of what to do next, she glanced out the window into the darkness. The inky blackness was impenetrable by the light coming from the room she was in, leaving the stars visible outside. Thousands of them. It had been a very long time since she'd seen the stars that bright. Living in Los Angeles most of her life, the city lights blanketed the sky with a dim light twenty-four hours a day. Occasionally she could hit the beach and see them, but with her job, she spent many a night chasing celebrities around the city trying to get interviews.

Rock Band News was the ultimate gig for her. She'd only been at the company about eight months and she'd spent six of those trying to get close to Iron Rogue. Shivers raced down her arms in excitement. She was standing in the home of Noah King. The frontman for the band and the one man no one had been able to get close to.

A soft knock on the door announced his arrival back into her room. "Here." He handed her a soft, light blue t-shirt. "It's not new or anything, but it should give you a little modesty. I'm quite a bit taller than you are, so it should hang long enough."

"It's great, Noah. Thank you again."

He backed toward the door. "I'll let you get some shut-eye. Catch you tomorrow, I guess. You can grab something in the kitchen before you lie down, if you like."

"I'll be right here in the morning and thank you for everything. I'll grab a bite before I lie down.."

The door closed softly behind him, leaving her to wonder again about the man. This was definitely not the guy everyone in the rock world knew. He had the reputation for being a hard ass, rough alcoholic who drank every chance he got, did drugs, partied with any woman he could get his hands on, and lived the ultimate rock star life. They didn't know the guy who owned an old farmhouse on some land who liked his privacy.

She couldn't wait to learn more.

Chapter Three

Sunlight poured through the gauzy curtains, sending a warm streak across Tori's cheek.

With her hands fisted and arms straight, she stretched her back across the soft as a cloud bed she'd slept on all night. Dreams of Noah's hands on her and his lips caressing her bare skin had kept her on edge. Even as the sun woke her this morning, her body hummed with pent-up energy and sexual frustration. Her experience with men wasn't something to write home about. The few guys she'd been with didn't seem to know what a woman wanted, much less needed to satisfy her to the point of toe curling.

Noah's reputation for being a womanizer left her wondering how much he knew in the satisfaction department.

She pushed her hair out of her face and sat up. *It doesn't matter. I'm not here to find my way into his bed. I am here to learn as much about the band as I can and print all the juicy details.*

Her toes hit the floor, bringing a screech to her lips. The plank floor beneath her feet was freezing. When she glanced down, she was shocked to see a pair of pink fuzzy slippers waiting at the side of the bed and a note on the nightstand.

Sorry about the freezing floor.
I hope these fit okay.
Bathroom has heated flooring.
Switch is by the door.

See you around lunch.
Noah

He brought me slippers? Wow.

The material was as soft as a fuzzy throw blanket, and the slippers fit her feet to perfection. How he knew her size, she wasn't sure, and how he got into the room and left them and the note, she didn't want to know. The thoughtfulness of his actions left her contemplating the rumor mill and the validity of their claims.

Spotting her clothing folded neatly on the dresser, she wondered again what he was up to. She obviously didn't have any clean clothes with her, but these were freshly washed.

He washed my clothes at two in the morning?

Grabbing her clothing in a rush, she raced into the bathroom to shower. The clock on the bedside table had read eleven. She wouldn't have much time if he would be back by lunch.

Steam filled the bathroom the moment she turned on the water and stripped off his t-shirt. The scent of sandalwood and male met her nose as she brought the material to her face. *Sniffing his shirt? Really?*

She laid it across the towel rack and stepped into the hot water.

Once she wet her hair, she realized he'd left travel size shampoo, conditioner, and soap inside the shower for her use, making her wonder how many women he brought here since he seemed so well stocked for company. Jealousy spiked hard inside her. *I don't have a reason to be jealous. He's not mine.*

The moment she finished her shower, she shut off the water and grabbed the towel on the rack. She needed to explore the house and the surrounding area to glean a bit of information before he came back from his morning errands. Information on Noah King was hers for the taking even if it made her feel like a bit of a lowlife sneaking around his house.

When she reached the kitchen a few minutes later, she found coffee hot on the counter with a bowl of sugar right next to it and creamer in another container. She also located a bowl and spoon with three boxes of cereal, Lucky Charms, which brought a giggle to her lips, Cheerios, and Captain Crunch. Apparently, Noah liked sugary cereals, too.

With a bowl of Lucky Charms in her fingers and a hot cup of coffee, she took a seat at the long farmhouse table. The table itself appeared to be handmade with long pine boards that were sanded smooth and polished with a very pretty walnut stain. The chairs were ladder-back and appeared to be handmade as well.

Sounds from outside were muted and peaceful. Birds chirped, cattle bawled low and loud, and very little other noise could be heard, no honking cars, no planes overhead, no people yelling, and no city noise. She couldn't wait to get outside to explore.

After she finished her breakfast, she washed out the bowl, cleaned the spoon, and put them in the cupboard before refilling her coffee and stepping outside through the kitchen door, the old wooden screen door banging shut behind her.

A long wood planked porch with turned spindle railings spanned the entire back side of the house. She took the two steps down and sat on the edge of the top stair to soak in the atmosphere. A call to Bella to let her know where she was in case something happened to her would be a good idea. Not that she thought anything would, but just to be safe

She pulled her phone from her pocket and hit the speed dial for her best friend in the world. The two of them had been inseparable since kindergarten and no one knew her better than Bella.

Her friend picked up on the second ring. "Hey, girl. How did the concert go last night? You had your big interview with Iron Rogue, right?"

"Hey, Bell. Yes and it went okay, I guess. Not like I'd hoped." Tori looped a piece of her hair around her finger, twirling absently while she looked over the backyard of Noah's house.

"That sucks."

"Yeah, but listen, I need to let you know I won't be home for a couple of weeks. I'm doing some in-depth stuff on the band."

Bella yelled at her dog to get down and then came back to the phone. "Sorry. In-depth? I'm not sure I understand."

Tori sighed for a second, not sure how much to reveal. Would it be taboo to tell her best friend she was at Noah King's house sitting on his back porch sipping coffee from one of his personal cups out of his private kitchen? "I'm in Iowa."

"Iowa? Like in corn fields and tractors Iowa?" she asked, disbelief clear in her voice.

"Yep, and home of Iron Rogue."

"You lost me, girl."

"I stowed away on the guy's plane last night. They were headed here, which is home for them, for a three-month break. Some personal shit for Noah, I think. I don't know for sure. I'm at his house right now."

A high-pitched scream almost broke her eardrum. "You have fucking got to be kidding me. You are at Noah King's house right this minute?"

"Yes. I'm sitting on the back porch."

"You have to be lying. No way."

"Yes way, and I am not lying. Want me to send you a picture? Although I'm not sure that's much proof. Noah isn't here at the moment."

"Oh my God!" She could hear rapid breathing through the phone.

"Breathe, Bella. It's okay."

"But…at Noah's house." A few more deep breaths. "Okay. Okay. I'm good. This is so fucking awesome!"

"You have to keep this under wraps, Bella. No one, and I mean absolutely no one, can know where I am. The guy's don't need that kind of publicity right now, and for me to get the information I need for the article, this has to be on the down low. Got it?"

"You bet, girl. You'll have to call me every day and let me know what's going on so I can live vicariously through you. And I hope to God you get laid by Noah King."

"Seriously, Bella? I'm not here to get laid by Noah or anyone else. I need this article and the information. If all I wanted was to get in his pants, I could have done that after the concert, I'm sure." She tucked a piece of hair behind her ear and shifted the phone to the other one. "You know how many women they have hanging on them all the time?"

"I know. I would give anything to be one of them."

"No you wouldn't. They probably don't even know the name of the last woman they slept with."

"Probably not, but to have any one of those guys between my thighs would be heaven on earth."

The picture of her best friend naked underneath Noah made her shiver in revulsion. She loved Bella with all her heart, but those images were something she didn't want or need. "Jesus. Okay. I have to go. I'm waiting for Noah to get back, and then I need to get this party started. I'll talk to you later. Oh, and don't expect a phone call every day. Ain't happening."

"Bye, sweetie. Have fun!"

"Bye."

The moment she hung up the phone, she sighed thinking about what she needed to do from here. The farmhouse was awesome and she couldn't wait to explore.

In the distance, she could see fencing surrounding a large section and several cattle munching on grass. To the right was a huge red barn, something she wanted to explore further. It had big doors that looked like they slid to the side to allow entrance, but also a smaller door that a person could walk through. A huge hay loft above looked inviting. She'd never been in one before.

To the left were fields of corn. It was early enough in the season the stocks were still very green and not too high yet. It was Iowa after all and most of their crops were corn.

Off to the right a little further, she could see some goats in a pen. They were really cute jumping around, up and down on what appeared to be a house. One in particular was brown and white, stood on top like he was king of the mountain. Another would knock him off every once in a while, but he'd get right back up there. A giggle escaped her lips as she watched.

* * * *

Noah stood in the doorway of the kitchen that led outside, leaning against the doorframe. Tori sat on the step with her coffee in hand, giggling like a child. He couldn't help but smile at her silliness. She sounded cute as she let herself enjoy the morning.

Her hair lay in soft waves around her shoulders, making his fingers itch to run through the silky strands. He'd left her shampoo and such in the shower this morning and the slippers by the bed, hoping she wouldn't be too inconvenienced by the unplanned trip to Iowa. They would need to get her some other things this morning, even if she had been the one to get herself in this situation.

His thoughts strayed to his trip to the home place. When he'd walked to his parents' house first thing that morning in order to let them know he was home, he'd been shocked by what he'd found. They wouldn't tell him until his sisters and brothers arrived later in the week, but he had a gut feeling something bad was going on. His father didn't look well. His gaunt and pale face told him a serious situation was at hand. Noah didn't want to know. He wasn't ready for his parents to be sick even though they were getting older. Neither of them was old enough to be terribly ill.

He cleared his throat and moved to sit beside her. "Enjoying the morning?"

When she glanced his way, he breath caught at the sight of her with those eyes bright and her face freshly clean with no makeup. It wasn't very often he saw a woman in his circles without her war paint on, dressed to the nines, and trying to impress him. Tori was gorgeous.

"I am. Thank you for the cereal and coffee. It was just what I needed to get me going. Did you go to your parents' place this morning?"

"Yeah." He looked out over his fields. The peaceful animal sounds and the breeze blowing through the corn fields settled his restless soul. "I let them know I was in town, but that was about it."

"Ah."

He climbed to his feet and held out his hand, waiting for her to place her palm in his. "We need to get you some stuff from town."

She hesitated a moment before she slid her hand into his. "Oh, yes we do." As soon as she was steady on her feet, she released his hand and stepped back. "Let me grab my tote bag and we'll go."

After she disappeared into the house, he went around to the front to start his truck. Shopping wasn't his forte, but he would take her where she needed to go to get some clothes and personal items. Summerton wasn't a big town. One department store, a drug store, a couple of cafes, and a gas station were about the extent of things available. The next town over wasn't much bigger.

"I'm ready," she said, bounding down the steps with a spring in her stride.

He held open the door on the passenger side as she climbed in, her lips lifting in a tempting smile as he closed it behind her.

"Where would you like to start first?" he asked, starting the truck and putting it into drive. "The department store in town has clothes and such. They should have about everything you need except shampoo and stuff."

"Perfect, Noah. I'll need a few outfits, jeans, shirts, shorts, and some under-things. Oh and something to sleep in. I can't use your shirt the whole time."

The thought of his shirt caressing her skin had him hard in an instant. He cleared his throat in a vain attempt to dislodge the knot that had formed. The vision of her wearing nothing but his shirt stuck in his brain. "No. Of course not."

It wasn't far to town, thank goodness, since the temperature in the truck had to have hit at least one hundred even with the air conditioner blasting.

"This is a really cute town. We didn't see much when we came through last night since it was so dark, but I like it. It is very quaint."

"I'm sure the mayor would love to hear your description." He glanced across the truck and was struck with how the sun reflected off her hair. He wanted to run his fingers through it just to see how soft it was. His fingers clung to the steering wheel in a death grip to keep from reaching for her. "As for most of us who are from here, it's a dot on the map and somewhere that we want to get away from the minute we can."

"Did you?" she asked, curiosity clear in her voice.

"Did I what?"

"Want to get away from here as soon as you could."

"Yes. The guys and I lit out of here the day after graduation." Bitterness tasted sour on his tongue. It was a long time ago, but he still felt like he'd deserted his family for his own selfish needs. "We had already been playing some of the clubs in the area, so we had some experience under our belts. We moved to Los Angeles and got an agent."

"From what I've been able to get with research, you guys hit it big pretty fast."

"We were damned lucky. Five years is fast in this business when there are hundreds that never even get a record deal. We actually didn't get ours until we had been playing for several years in L.A."

They pulled into the department store parking lot, and he shut off the truck. The engine made a slow ticking sound as it cooled.

"Your song was the breaking point for Iron Rogue."

"Yeah, it was." He pushed open the door and stepped out.

She met him around the front of the vehicle. "Shall we?"

"I'm not much of a shopper."

He followed her into the store and then toward the back where it appeared the women's section lay.

"I am," she said with a smile. "You just sit in the corner and look like the hot rock star, okay?"

He found a large chair near the dressing room doors and slid down into it. With his ankles crossed and his fingers laced across his stomach, he watched her flit from one rack to another. A pink tank top made it to her growing pile held by one finger. Multiple shirts, tanks, and jeans were in her arms as she came toward the dressing room.

A sales girl who had been hovering nearby, stepped forward with her eyes wide and a nervous grin on her lips. "Aren't you Noah King of Iron Rogue?"

His gaze met Tori's as he sighed. This was one of those things he hated. Most of the people in this area didn't think twice about him or the band because they'd grown up here. To them, they weren't celebrities. This girl, he didn't know. "Yes."

A high-pitched squeal left her lips as she rushed closer. "Oh my God! I am a huge fan. One of my friends told me you lived here but since I'd never seen you, I thought she was lying. Can I get a picture?" she asked, pulling out her cell phone from God knows where. Her outfit left little to the imagination with her skin-tight mini-skirt and flowing spaghetti strapped tank top. She couldn't be more than sixteen.

"Uh, yeah, sure." He stood up and let the girl get in close as she snapped a photo with her phone. "Now, can you help my friend here and let her into the dressing rooms, please? She needs some clothes."

"Oh yes, of course." The girl took the key from around her wrist and opened the door. "You can use number four." Her gaze went from Noah to Tori. "Um, since you are with Noah, you can take however many in there you want."

Tori shook her head, rolling her eyes a little before she stepped inside and closed the door.

He took his seat again and pulled out his phone, hoping the girl would leave them alone now that he'd done his duty and took a picture with her. Every few moments he'd glance up from his screen to find the sales girl staring at him from over the top of some of the clothes racks. When he'd catch her looking, she'd scurry off in another direction until he caught her again. *This kind of stuff is irritating as hell.*

A moment later, Tori came out wearing skinny jeans that hugged every curve of her hips and ass, a white gauzy shirt tied at the waist and a black tank top under it that emphasized the slope of her breast until his mouth watered to trace the line of the shirt. *Holy hell!*

"Well? What do you think? Simple enough for Summerton, Iowa?"

He felt like he'd swallowed his tongue as he climbed to his feet to admire the look on her. Surely the damned thing would unstick from the roof of his mouth to be able to talk. "Wow."

"Wow good or wow bad?"

"Good." *Breathe man, breathe.* "I mean, you look great!"

Her cheeks flushed with color that looked absolutely gorgeous on her. "Thanks. This stuff isn't too pricey, so I can get several outfits without hurting my budget too much."

"Don't worry about the prices. I'll cover it."

She shook her head, her hair moving slightly across her shoulders. "No, Noah. I'm here because I stowed away on your plane. You didn't want me here. It isn't right for you to pay for my clothes."

He shoved his hands into the front pockets of his jeans, to keep from touching her, a nervous habit he'd gained since meeting her. "I want to. It was my idea for you to spend some time here to learn about us as normal people. I'll buy your clothes."

"I can't accept such a generous gift. I will pay you back then."

"We can discuss it later. For now, I will take care of the bill for the clothes. Consider it a gift."

"A gift for what?"

He shrugged, hoping it didn't look as adolescent as it felt. "For putting up with me for the next two weeks."

With a grin on her lips, she turned on her heels and disappeared back into the dressing room. *What in the hell have I gotten myself into?*

After three hours of shopping for everything Tori would need to spend two weeks in Iowa, he rushed her off to the local café for some food. His stomach had been growling for a bit, and Bushes Place had the best food in town. Besides, they wouldn't make a big deal of his presence. He'd known Margie and Bill since before he could walk.

The bell dinged over the door as he pushed it open and held it for Tori. The place hadn't changed much in twenty years. The red vinyl booths still lined the wall to the right under the windows and the long eat-in bar still sat to the left where many of the locals hung out with their coffee cups grasped between their hands.

"Noah!" Margie rushed toward him, wrapping him in a big, warm hug. "You look gorgeous as usual." She peered at Tori. "And who is this pretty lady?"

"Margie, this is Tori. She's a friend who's visiting for a couple of weeks."

"Well, it's nice to meet you, Tori." She grabbed her hand. "Come, let's find the perfect table for you two."

Noah shook his head as Margie dragged Tori to the booth in the back corner. The one he always sat in when he was home, and the one he'd carved his name into the table right before he left for Los Angeles to make it big.

"What can I get you two to drink?"

"Coke is fine for me," Tori replied.

"Me too."

"Coming right up." A few moments later, Margie disappeared behind the counter.

"You'll have to excuse her. She's known me for years."

Tori grinned. "I gathered that. I think it's sweet."

Heat crept up his cheeks as he looked at the menu that hadn't changed since he'd left.

When Margie returned with their Cokes, she said, "Roast Beef with potatoes and gravy on special today."

Tori closed her menu and put it back inside the rack at the head of the table behind the napkins. "Oh, that sounds wonderful."

"Make it two."

Margie placed her hand on his cheek. "You look tired, Noah. I hope you get some rest while you're home. All that touring will wear you out."

"I hope so, too, but something is going on at home and I'm here to deal with it."

"Nothing bad, I hope." Margie's gaze turned serious and thoughtful as she glanced from him to Tori.

"I'm not sure yet. Mom and Dad aren't saying anything until the others get home at the end of the week."

"If you need anything you holler, okay?"

"Yes, ma'am."

"Be right back with those plates."

Noah glanced at Tori across the table, his gaze caught on the shiny strands of her hair, the softness of her skin, and the dimple in her cheek when she smiled.

"What are you looking at?"

"Nothing." He shifted his sight to her hands, fragile yet capable. "Did you bring a notepad to write stuff down as you saw things?"

"Yes," she said, grabbing at her large bag next to her on the seat.

Pen to paper, she began to scribble some notes on the pad as they waited for their food, and he watched her. Her brow crinkled, spreading small lines across her forehead, when she concentrated. She stuck her tongue out and to the side of her mouth while she wrote very quickly across the paper.

He chuckled under his breath, causing her to raise her head.

"What's so funny?"

"Nothing, really. I think it's cute how you concentrate."

Her eyes narrowed as a frown pulled down the corners of her mouth. "Cute?"

"Yeah."

Margie arrived with their food, causing Tori to move the paper to the side. Noah wanted to read what she'd written so badly he could taste it.

"This looks great, Margie," Tori said, as she dug her fork into the potatoes.

"Thank you, sweetie. It's one of my favorites." Her gaze turned to Noah. "You need to put some meat on those bones, son. You're too skinny."

"I've always been too skinny for you, Margie. I could weigh three hundred pounds and I'd be too skinny for you."

Margie laughed, a big loud gawf that made the whole room smile. "This is true. Eat up!" With a pat on his shoulder, she disappeared back behind the counter.

Lord, he loved that lady.

While they ate, he kept glancing at Tori. She wasn't like other women who hardly ate anything when they were out with a guy. Food appeared to be something she enjoyed. Her body was gorgeous the way it was, all curvy in the right places. His palms itched to grab ahold of those curves and trace every one of them with his tongue. *I need to pull my head out from between her thighs otherwise this is going to get deep.* "So, where did you grow up, Victoria?" He liked the way her given name rolled off his tongue.

A frown marred her pretty face. "Call me Tori, please. My Dad calls me Victoria when I'm in trouble."

"It sounds like an old family name."

"It is. It was my grandmother's on my dad's side. She's been gone for about twenty years. She died when I was seven."

He took a huge bite of his roast beef, chewing slowly as he contemplated this little bit of information. *More.* "That makes you twenty-seven."

"Yep."

"Let's see. What else can I find out?" She wore several rings on her fingers, but none on the ring finger of her left hand. *Not married.* A tattoo on her right shoulder played peek-a-boo with him. "I am assuming you are a fan of rock."

A green bean found its way between her straight white teeth. "I listen to a lot of different types of music including classical, country, old rock mostly from the eighties and nineties, as well as the current stuff."

"Where were you born?"

Her green eyes narrowed as she focused on his face. Today, she wore no makeup at all since she'd come with them to Iowa with nothing. She didn't need it though. Her complexion was flawless with no blemishes anywhere he could see, although she had a small mole on the side of her cheek near her ear that he hadn't noticed last night. A smattering of freckles ran over her nose and across her cheeks, giving her a much younger appearance than her twenty-seven years. She'd pulled her hair back in a low ponytail near the base of her neck, letting it lay down her back in soft waves. He liked the way she looked, probably too much.

"What kind of game are you playing, Noah?"

"Game?"

"Keep me from asking you questions by making me tell my life story?" She pushed her potatoes around her plate before laying the fork down beside it. "Fine, we can do this. If I tell you mine, then you have to tell me yours."

"The plan is for you to learn everything about us, Victoria. It will be much easier for me to give you what you want to know if I have a few secrets on you as well."

"You want secrets, huh?"

"Isn't that what you want from me?" He leaned back against the booth, resting his arm across the back. Secrets were a way of life for a rock star, and he knew how to play the game like an expert.

A small smile lifted the corners of her mouth. "Maybe. I'm sure your fans would love to know a few things about you they don't already know and I'm here to give it to them."

"Then turnabout is fair play, right?" Their verbal sparring was more fun than he'd imagined. "Tell me the one thing about you that no one knows, a secret wish, something you've done you are embarrassed about—it can be anything, but it has to be a deep, personal secret."

It took her several minutes while he watched the emotions run across her face. Her eyes changed colors several times from moss green to seafoam green during the process. The moment she came to what she would tell him, a mischievous grin spread across her face, and her eyes turned a spring grass green.

She leaned forward, whispering so only the two of them could hear. "Sometimes, when I'm all alone and taking a nice warm bath with lots of bubbles, I will put on some music and let myself go. Do you want to know what song I listen to?"

"Yeah," he breathed, his pants getting tighter by the second as he imagined her naked in a bath, bubbles caressing her shoulders and neck.

Her voice had a breathy quality that almost had him coming in his pants. God help him, he was in deep.

"That really deep, low part you sing in Dare to Love, where you whisper the words, *forever my love.*"

Chapter Four

Noah's pupil's dilated as he contemplated what she said. She could tell he wanted to respond with something smart, but he wasn't sure whether to be turned on or shocked. His fingers were curled under like he was trying to hold it together.

A giggle almost escaped as she leaned back against the vinyl seat and stuck a fork full of potatoes into her mouth, rolling the soft concoction around on her tongue.

All this sexual tension between them had her on edge and heat thrumming through her veins like rushing molten lava. Turning the tables on him was fun. He needed to lighten up a bit. Serious didn't work on him.

His breath came out rather fast while his gaze lingered on her face, dropping to her lips for a second before returning to her eyes. "Do you."

"Uh-huh, and you know what else?" she whispered, leaning toward him.

"What?"

"My orgasms are pretty intense when I do that."

Noah coughed slightly as he covered his mouth, hiding a grin he couldn't help. "Dirty girl."

"Yep." What made her be so open with him, she didn't know, but she kind of liked sparring with him. Conversations were fun when they weren't so serious. "Now tell me a secret about you?"

His gaze shifted to something over her shoulder. A frown tugged at his lips, drawing them down at the corners. His shoulders pulled back slightly and his hands rest beside the plate in front of him.

She could tell he contemplated what to say, knowing he didn't want to spill anything personal. It was too early in their weird relationship. His fans wanted to know about him, anything they could get their hands on, but it had to be something they didn't already know. His first kiss? When he'd lost his virginity? How had it felt the first time he'd been on stage? Did he get stage fright during a show?

When he focused back on her face, a small smile lifted his lips in a crooked grin. "I got a speeding ticket the night of my senior prom. I was in such a hurry to get my date home because I had the perfect beginning lyric for Dare to Love, I had to write it down. I ended up staying up all night sitting in my room, still in my tux, writing down the lyrics. The whole song was done that night."

"You wrote the lyrics to the entire song in one sitting?"

He nodded as one eyebrow shot up over his left eye. "Yes. I even had the melody in my head so I called Alex and sang it to him over the phone. He wasn't very appreciative since he was in the middle of having sex with his date."

A laugh bubbled from her lips as she jotted down notes on her pad. This was the type of information she needed for her article. Alex had sex at prom, but Noah didn't. *Perfect.* "Did your date get pissed?"

"Yeah, a bit. We didn't see each other again after that night."

"So you are saying the lyrics from Dare to Love had to do with your lack of feelings for her?" She held her breath. He would reveal the one thing everyone wanted to know.

"What? No. I mean, not really." His face flushed under his tan as his gaze darted around them. "Leave it alone, Tori. Those lyrics are personal, very personal, and I will not talk about them to you or anyone," he growled before scooting out of the booth, grabbing the check Margie had left on the table, and marching to the cash register.

Her mouth hung open for a moment as she watched him. Levi's clung to his lean hips, a dark t-shirt molded to his sculpted back, and his long black hair hung to his waist, leaving every woman in the room wondering what it would be like to have the intensity of his personality focused on them. His frustration was evident in his stride and jerky movements. He did *not* want to talk about that song. Unfortunately, Tori was determined to get the scoop on the very thing he didn't want to talk about.

When he turned back around, his eyes were narrowed and a frown tugged at his lips. "Come on."

He didn't wait for her to follow as he pushed open the door to the café, letting it slam shut in her face. She hurried after him, trying to keep up with his rapid footsteps. "Noah, wait." She clutched his arm, wrapping her fingers around the taut muscles. "I'm sorry if I dug too deep."

His gaze met hers. "Leave it alone, Tori."

He continued on until he reached his truck. She didn't wait for him to open the door, just climbed in, afraid he'd leave her behind.

Without another word, he started the vehicle, put it in drive, and headed out of town. Unsure where they were going, Tori held on as she watched the scenery buzz by.

Noah stayed quiet. The only sound in the truck was the radio playing some old rock. Everything around them seemed a typical Iowa farm town. Fields and fields of corn were planted on both sides of the road with a house tucked back amongst the green stalks every few miles. Huge pieces of machinery stood waiting like silent sentinels.

As cars and trucks passed them on the road, occasionally someone would honk and Noah would wave in recognition.

"Do you know everyone?"

"I've lived here all my life. I grew up with most of these people. Just because I play in a band, doesn't mean these people aren't important to me." His voice was low and gruff. Pissed off didn't even come close to the emotions he was giving off.

Leaving their conversation alone for a few moments, she decided to tempt his rage by stating a fact she'd noticed. "You are so different from what I thought you'd be."

"You mean I'm not a stuck up rock star?"

"You seem like a normal person."

"Traveling and having money, Tori, most of the time leaves you very lonely. Yes, there are women at every venue willing to sleep with you because you're a rock star, but when you wake up next to one and you can't even remember her name, that life gets old."

"I hadn't thought of that." The life he described did seem lonely and cold. She'd always thought having money would be great. Go where you wanted, when you wanted. People busting their asses to serve you. Traveling to faraway places. Somehow she didn't think it was so great anymore.

Noah glanced across the truck, his fingers silently tapping out the rhythm of the song on the radio before focusing his gaze back out the windshield.

"Where we going?"

"I'm taking you to my parents' place. I thought that would be a good place to start in your quest to learn about the real me."

Excitement zipped along her nerves. This is what she had come to Iowa for. Finally, she would have something on him that no one else knew.

Several minutes later, they drove down a long gravel road with fenced pasture on each side. Horses and cattle grazed in the distance, spotting the landscape with their black and white coats against the green of the grass. Peaceful.

The house came into view, taking her breath away. It wasn't fancy by any means, but it looked like home. White clapboard siding with red trim and a red roof and a long porch gave her the feeling of the place being loved by those who lived there. White curtains blew in the breeze of the open windows. A multitude of colored flowers grew along the foundations and around the walkways leading to the back of the house. The porch went along the front, giving plenty of room for rocking chairs and lazing on the steps in the afternoon sun.

"This is gorgeous, Noah. Is this where you grew up?"

"Yeah. I spent a lot of time on horseback out in those pastures and playing guitar in the barn."

"You play?"

"Some. Nothing like the guys in the band. I can pick enough to get by and write, but that's about it."

Mental note. Noah plays guitar!

An older woman with graying hair pulled back in a long ponytail at the base of her neck stepped out on the porch. She was thin, very thin from what Tori could tell, but her eyes were bright and clear with understanding and love as Noah stepped from the truck.

Her arms were out, welcoming her son into a tight hug. "I didn't know you were coming back this afternoon."

"I brought a friend, Mom." He turned toward Tori. "Mom, this is Tori. Tori, this is my mother, Eileen."

Tori held out her hand, grasping the frail woman's fingers. "It's very nice to meet you. Thank you for welcoming me to your home."

"Any friend of Noah's is welcome here, sweetie." Her gaze narrowed on Tori's face a moment before she turned back toward her son. "I just made some sweet tea. Why don't we get some and sit on the porch? It's a beautiful day already."

"I'll get it, Mom. You sit down and rest a bit. You look tired."

"Thanks, honey. I have been up since early. You know your dad. Off to the fields no matter what is going on, so he's had his breakfast, his coffee, and is on the tractor."

Noah shook his head as he guided his mom to the rocker in the corner. "Sit. I'll be right back."

Eileen held out her hand, shooing Tori toward one of the chairs. "Come sit with me, Tori. I don't get much female company out here. It's just me and Noah's dad now that the kids are grown and gone."

Tori took the chair to her right, pushing her toe against the floor to set the rocker in motion. The slow rhythmic motion soothed her soul, making her realize how tense and strung out she'd been lately. Her life was crazy at times, running here and there, chasing rock stars for their interviews, hardly ever home, missing her friend, and staying up late nights to get her articles done. "It's a beautiful home. You must be very proud."

Eileen's gaze focused out over the pasture before returning to Tori's face, a small smile lifting the corners of her mouth. Noah's mother was a beautiful woman in her own right, but life had taken its toll. She had fine lines near her eyes and mouth that came with age even though she couldn't be more than in her mid-fifties. "It's my home. We've lived here for a very long time." She patted Tori's hand. "How did you meet my Noah?"

Heat crawled up Tori's face as embarrassment rushed through her. She still couldn't believe she'd been crazy enough to stow away on their private plane. "Well, I'm a reporter, and I was assigned to do an article on Iron Rogue. I was at their last show. Their fans want to know some personal tidbits."

Eileen's eyes crinkled at the corners as she started to laugh. Tears rolled down her cheeks while the giggles continued.

The screen door banged shut as Noah came out carrying three glasses of sweet tea. "What's so funny?"

Noah's mother dabbed at her cheeks. "Tori just informed me of her assignment and knowing how private you are, I find it hilarious."

Tori frowned. She didn't think it was funny at all. This was her job and she took it seriously. Digging up the dirt on Noah and the guys would cement her career. "Noah actually invited me to come to Iowa so I could learn a few things about him and the band."

"You did?" Eileen glanced at Noah, mirth still clear in her eyes.

"Yeah. Well sort of. She stowed away on the plane. Rather than take her back, I thought it would be a good idea for her to see the real us. She gets her article, and maybe they'll leave us alone for a while." He handed a glass to each of the women before taking a seat on the bench swing.

Studying him for a moment, she noticed the lines around his mouth and eyes were less pronounced. Peace radiated from him as he sipped his tea and gently swung back and forth. It seemed clear he loved it here. "The guys will get to read the article before it's published, that way there won't be any surprises when it hits the newsstands."

The rattle of a diesel tractor got louder and louder as it came closer to the front porch. An older gentleman perched on the yellow seat waved his arm in greeting as he shut the engine off and climbed down, before taking the two steps up to the porch. He leaned over Noah's mother and left a peck of a kiss on her lips. "Good afternoon, my love." After he lovingly touched her cheek, he turned toward Noah enveloping him in a warm hug. "Son. It's good to see you back at the house. When you came by this morning, I didn't realize you'd be back so soon."

"Dad, this is Tori. Tori, this is my dad Wayne."

"Nice to meet you, Tori. Are you a friend of Noah's?"

"Yes, she is, Dad."

"Wonderful. He rarely brings friends here, other than the boys from the band."

Noah's dad had lines upon lines around his mouth and eyes, making him look much older than she would have guessed. His hands were large with apparent calluses upon calluses, and his chest was broad as were his shoulders. He looked very capable of taking on anything he wanted to. She could see where Noah got his height and build although his father didn't look well. "Thank you for the wonderful welcome to your home, sir."

"No sir needed, young lady. We're just Wayne and Eileen around here," he said, taking Eileen's hand. "Mama, can I refill your sweet tea?"

"I would love some more, Papa."

Noah climbed to his feet. "I'll get it."

Tori could see sweat glistening on Wayne's forehead as he dabbed at his neck and face with his handkerchief. The color of his skin seemed off. He wasn't necessarily pale, but the hue of his complexion looked almost yellow.

"Thank you, son. I appreciate it," he said with a sigh as he took the other empty rocker on the porch.

"No problem, Dad."

As Noah disappeared back into the house, Tori watched the interaction between Wayne and Eileen. They were obviously very much in love even though they'd been together a number of years. She couldn't really decide their ages, though she knew Noah was the oldest, and he was thirty-two based on her research. They did have a large family from what she knew, with four boys and two girls. Two of the boys were twins and all of them were fairly close in age. Controlled chaos around the ranch when they were little, she imagined. "Do your other children live around here?"

Eileen patted her husband's hand. "Our daughters live in the next town over with their husbands and children. The twins are off chasing their fortune in California, and our other boy lives near us besides Noah. I guess you're staying at his house?" Eileen pushed a strand of hair behind her ear, her gaze open and curious.

"Yes. He invited me to stay with him while I'm here. In the guest bedroom."

Eileen's eyes crinkled at the corners as she smiled. Tori wasn't sure if that meant she believed her or not. It didn't matter. Getting involved with Noah was a really bad idea, even if her body was completely onboard with finding out just how good he was in bed.

Noah returned with Eileen's glass and the pitcher of tea. "I brought it with me just in case someone else needed a refill."

Tori raised her glass, her gaze meeting Noah's as she silently asked for more. The heated intensity in his eyes when they met hers spoke volumes on the tension between them. She knew he felt it too.

"Why don't you show Tori around the place, Noah?"

"I would love that." She set her now empty glass on the porch and climbed to her feet.

"Wonderful," Eileen exclaimed as she climbed to her feet with a little wobble and a weary sigh as she headed for the screen door. "I need to get started on supper anyway. You two will be staying for supper, right?"

"We actually just ate, Mom," Noah replied.

Eileen waved her hand as if shooing them off to do whatever they wanted. "Oh, it won't be ready for several hours. I'm making a roast and it takes a while to cook."

Noah took Tori's hand in his, much to her surprise, and led her down the porch steps. "Good, then will be back in a little while."

A path along the side of the house led out toward the pasture. Gravel crunched under their feet until they reached the edge and through a small metal cattle gate. Early cornstalks pushed from the rich earth reaching for the warming sun, for miles and miles. The scent of fresh-tilled dirt permeated the air as they made their way out toward a cluster of trees in the distance, which seemed to be their destination. "Where we going?" she asked, enjoying the heat of the sun on her skin.

"I'm showing you my home."

The warmth of his hand where it grasped hers gave way to fantasies she wasn't sure she wanted to put a name to. Heat simmered under her skin, tingling down her nerves from where they touched clear to her toes. Thoughts of those palms running along the outside of her thighs as they made their way toward her hips had her shivering in the temperature.

"Chilled?"

"No. Excited to see where we're going." *Good save.*

As they broke through the trees, a small pool of water gurgled in front of them, surrounded by boulders and bushes of junipers. The trickle of a stream was like a tinkle of the high notes on the xylophone, barely discernible except for the quiet surrounding them. Birds flitted from tree to tree, twittering to their mates. "This is gorgeous, Noah."

"It's one of my favorite spots. I used to come here a lot when I was a kid."

Noah led her to a large boulder with a large flat side where they could sit and dangle their feet in the water. The coolness of the water gave her chills that raced up her legs. The feeling was fabulous and enchanting to the city girl inside her.

They sat in silence for a few moments as she took in his profile, loving the slope of his nose and the fullness of his lips. She'd never been attracted to a man with a beard, but his looked soft to the touch, perfectly framing his sensuous lips. She cleared her throat to forestall those wayward thoughts that wouldn't be good for either one of them. "Why don't you tell me about your siblings? I understand you have three brothers and two sisters, with two of the brothers being twins."

He didn't answer for a few minutes, his gaze fixed out over the water. "My brother's names are Ben, Elijah, and Daniel. I am the oldest, then Ben. My sisters are Sophie and Mia. The twins are the youngest, Elijah and Daniel." A slow exhale of breath gave her nothing of his thoughts.

"What was it like growing up with a big family?"

When he turned to face her, she could see the love for his family in his eyes, those dark soulful eyes. Did he realize how bare his soul was to her in that gaze?

"We had a lot of fun when I was a kid. Ben and I were very close. We used to get in trouble all the time. After I started the band, we drifted apart. I was always practicing with the guys, so it didn't leave a lot of time for him."

He reached out, his fingers capturing a stray piece of hair that had drifted across her cheek before he tucked it behind her ear. The touch of his fingertips on her skin had a shiver rolling down her back. She wanted more. What she wouldn't give for the feel of his hands buried in her hair, cupping the back of her neck, as his mouth drifted closer. "Are you protective of your sisters?"

A low rumble of laughter left his lips. "Of course. Their respective husbands had to run the gauntlet before we would ever let them go out with him." He pulled his feet from the water, moving back a little so he rested on his hands. "Don't get me wrong, they both have great spouses and their kids are just cute. I don't get to see them as much as I'd like. With all the traveling we do, it's hard to get together." His hair drifted on a slight breeze, lifting the ends as he looked back out over the water, his silence more telling than anything he'd already said. He really was a complicated individual.

After several moments, she said, "I don't mean to pry, but your dad doesn't look well."

He turned toward her, capturing her gaze with his. Fear and sorrow told her he didn't like what was happening to his family although he didn't know exactly what to fear. "Yeah, I noticed. I'm not sure what's up with them. They called us all home for some reason. They haven't told me what's going on yet. They're waiting until my brothers and sisters get here."

Touching his hand, she hoped to bring him a little peace. "I hope everything will be okay."

"We shall see, I guess." He glanced down at where her fingers were. "What do you like to do for fun, Tori?" Laughter glinted in his eyes as well as something deeper, something stronger, something more. "Except for giving yourself an orgasm to my voice."

Heat raced up from her chest in embarrassment. She should never have told him that. "Well, I like to swim, play pool, listen to music, and hang out with rock stars." She grabbed her shoes, slipping them back on before climbing to her feet and walked away, needing a moment to gather her racing thoughts and calm down her libido. A large flat rock to her left gave her a stunning view of the pasture laid out before her. The trees overhead kept it cooler in the shade, affording her a respite from the scorching heat. Cattle dotted the landscape far off in the distance, separated from the corn, black dots on the otherwise green of the landscape. Open land as far as she could see left her calm and relaxed unlike the hustle and bustle of the city. She could do this kind of atmosphere.

Noah walked up behind her, letting his hands fall to her shoulders. The warmth of his body penetrated her t-shirt, heating her skin, scorching her until she felt like she would burn alive. The need to turn around and bury her face in his shoulder overwhelmed her with its intensity. If she gave into that need, she would drown in him.

His fingers moved her hair away from her neck in a soft brush of skin. Want and need shot through her veins like molten lava, slowly eating her alive from the inside. His hot breath fanned her flesh as he brushed the curve between her neck and her shoulder with his lips. Goosebumps chased the movement of his fingertips down her arm, scattering across her flesh as if it was buzzing.

He took her hand, turning her to face him. When she looked up, his eyes had turned dark, seeming to search hers for the answer to why now or why us.

One finger traced along her jaw before his hand slid beneath her hair at the nape of her neck, drawing her toward him in a slow, measured movement meant to give her the choice to stop this now or allow him to devour her.

Her breathing sputtered and then stopped as she waited for his lips to descend, capturing hers in the kiss she'd wanted since the moment she'd met him.

His other hand came up to capture the other side of her face as he angled her head to deepen the kiss. His tongue flicked out, asking for permission as it slipped along the seam of her lips. With a deep moan, she opened her mouth allowing his tongue inside. His ate at her mouth, taking and giving at the same time. Whimpers of need escaped while he continued his sensual assault on her, making her realize her whole world had narrowed to this one moment in time, this one kiss. She clung to his wrists, hoping he would never stop his onslaught of her senses. This kiss would haunt her memories for the rest of her life.

It seemed like it went on forever, but not long enough as he finally raised his head. "I should not get involved with you, Tori. This could end so badly for you."

"What if I'm willing to take that chance?"

"What if I'm not?" His gaze searched hers for a second before he grasped her hand and they headed back down toward his parents' house.

Unsure of how to proceed, she followed him silently, picking their way along the trail although he never let go of her hand.

Her thoughts were in turmoil, rolling around in her head without meaning or purpose other than Noah had kissed her senseless.

A toss of her head brought her mind back into a little focus. Where should she go from here? She was really beginning to like him, a lot. From what she knew, he had a lot of demons. Did she really know him? All she had were rumors, hearsay, did she give him the benefit of the doubt?

Who was the real Noah King?

Chapter Five

Noah paced his room later that night, his steps taking him back and forth in front of the window overlooking the back of the house. "What the hell was I thinking? I do not need to get involved with Tori. Yes, she seems like a nice girl, and she's sexy as hell with those pouty lips, big sexy eyes, and that killer body. But she's so not what I need in my life, especially right now."

His fingers left track marks through his hairline as he pushed them repeatedly through the long strands before becoming frustrated and pulling it back into a tie.

Water coming on behind the bathroom door drew his gaze to the closed portal between his room and Tori's. *Fuck me. She's in the shower.* His cock rose to the occasion as he pictured her naked body standing under the spray. This was the last thing he needed tonight after getting a taste of her earlier.

Her lips had been soft and luscious under his and the moment she'd released that sexy little moan he'd been gone. It had taken every ounce of self-control, something he didn't usually worry about using, to lift his head.

Before he knew it, his steps had taken him to the bathroom door. He braced his hands on each side of the doorway and hung his head. The need to feel her beneath him was almost more than he could handle. The burn of need spiked hard along the base of his spine.

The soft humming of a song reached his ears. The melody sounded familiar. It should. It was the chords of Dare to Love.

As her voice became softer near the end of the song, Tori's words came back to his mind, and he leaned closer to the door. Was what she'd said true? Did she really orgasm to the sound of his voice? Leaning so he was almost press to the door, Noah could hear her breathlessness, his own breathing becoming choppy while he listened.

Unaware of his hand turning the doorknob, he slowly pushed the door open revealing the goddess from his fantasies over the last several nights.

Tori had her head thrown back, her left hand flat on the glass shower stall, one foot braced on the shower seat, and her right hand buried between her thighs. Her lips moved silently saying the last words of the song over and over.

He needed to be the one bringing her pleasure.

Quickly removing his clothes, he stepped into the shower and pressed his lips to the base of her neck as his hands cupped her breasts. Desire twisted hot in his gut. His cock slid along the crack of her ass as he plucked and pulled at her nipples, bringing them to tight points.

His name rushed from her lips in a whisper, questioning his presence. "Noah?"

"No questions. No promises," he murmured, turning her toward him so he could see her face.

Hot water beat down on his head as he skimmed his lips over her collarbone, tasting her skin, learning what turned her on. Her hands rested on his shoulders while he continued to map the curves and dips of her body. She was magnificent. Her breasts were a nice handful, perfect in his palms, with rose-colored nipples just begging for his mouth. Her waist curved gently down to nicely round hips and a killer ass. She was everything perfect in a woman.

A soft moan escaped her lips the moment he took her nipple in his mouth, rubbing it with his tongue. Using his teeth to bring a little pain had her coming up on her toes and a sexy little whimper passing through her parted lips. Her body shook as he moved his right hand between her thighs, glancing off her clit before sliding his finger over one side and then the other.

"Oh, God."

Her hand moved between them, sliding down his chest until she encircled his cock with her warm palm. A gasp and a moan followed by a whole body shudder made him wonder at his reaction for a moment. Pleasure with sex was a given for him, but this was something totally different. He'd never responded so acutely to anyone. "Be careful. That's loaded."

Her lips lifted in a cute little smile. "I'm counting on it."

The water began to cool, so he shut the spigot off, grabbed the towel hanging over the door and dried her off from her long hair to her cute pink toenails. Once he had himself dry, he took her hand and led her into his room, stopping next to the king-sized bed.

Using both hands, he cupped her face, smoothing his thumbs over her cheekbones as he stared into the depths of her eyes. Little flecks of gold memorized him for a second. "You are so beautiful. I could stare at you all day."

She turned her face, kissing his palm, the movement sensual and sweet at the same time.

"Are you sure you're okay with this?"

"I want you, Noah. I have since I met you, rock star and all." She brushed her lips over his. "No promises."

He pressed his forehead against hers for a moment, taking in everything about her from her tempting mouth to her sparkling eyes, she was fantastic. The moment his mouth found hers, he was lost. The sensations bombarding him left him breathless, each one more potent than the next. His cock strained painfully against his abdomen, his balls heavy against his thigh, wanting her with every breath. His heart pounded in his chest, the rapid beat thudding so hard he thought it might pop right out of his ribcage.

She turned toward the bed, throwing him a wicked little grin over her shoulder as she pulled down the covers and crawled into the middle, beaconing him with a crook of her finger.

As he moved toward her, she slid down so her head rested on the pillow never used on the other side of the bed. It seemed right for her to be there. Her gorgeous hair fanned out on the pillow still wet from the shower, but he didn't care. This was Tori, in his bed, hopefully for at least a few days. He wouldn't think beyond that. He couldn't.

His lips met hers, stealing her sighs and giving them back. Her skin felt cool to his touch. Goosebumps peppered her skin. "Cold?"

Her hands wandered up his sides, sliding across his skin in a sexy dance of her fingers. "Warm me up. I want all of you. Every inch."

"You got it, babe," he whispered, his lips moving over her cheek to skim down her neck. Her scent was something he couldn't place. Sweet yet uniquely Tori. Her skin tasted salty beneath his tongue while he continued his assault on her senses, touching her with his fingertips to heighten every sensation he could get from her. He wanted it all.

A soft moan sounded in his ear as he moved down to take a nipple between his lips, pulling at the tip until it stood to a hard point. He bit down, just enough to cause her a little pain. God, he loved the sounds coming from her mouth. Every whimper, every sigh, every breathless hitch made him harder than he'd ever been in his life.

Moving down her abdomen, kissing each freckle and each curve, he reached the top of her mound. A subtle parting of her thighs let him know what she wanted. He was happy to oblige, needing to taste her sweetness on his tongue.

The first flick against her clit made her hips come off the bed. "Noah," she breathed, saying his name on a prayer.

When he pushed two fingers into her hot center, the tightness surrounding him had his cock hard enough to pound steel. He couldn't wait to get inside her and feel all of that around him.

A few swipes of his tongue as he slid his fingers in and out of her had her screaming his name within a few short moments. Her essence coated his tongue. She tasted like heaven, not something he would soon forget.

He kissed his way back up her body before reaching over to the bedside table drawer and pulling out a condom.

Her questioning gaze remained on his face until he held up a silver package. A small nod of her head let him know she was onboard with his use of a condom. He never went without one with *any* woman. He couldn't afford the complications should something happen. Not that he didn't trust her, strange enough he probably trusted her too much, but accidents happen and he certainly didn't need a kid right now.

The moment he had the protection in place, he brought their lips together, deepening the kiss as he slowly slid inside her. It seemed like a hundred sensations bombarded him all at once. The slick heat wrapped around him like a fist. The tightness of her had him holding his breath and counting slowly to keep from coming too quickly. Shooting his load like a teenager wouldn't endear her to him in the least.

Sexy little moans vibrated along his lips as he continued to kiss her while he slowly fucked her. *It's fucking. It's fucking.* Being with her like this seemed right, more right than anything else ever had.

He felt the tug of her fingers at the base of his neck, undoing where he tied his hair. Bearing his weight on his arms, he lifted his chest off of her allowing his hair to become an inky curtain around them.

With the shift of his body, he brought her up in front of him as he pushed back on his haunches, never losing their connection.

Her arms wrapped around his neck, pulling his lips to hers. He guided her hips so she could ride his cock until they were both breathless and moaning each other's names. "So wet. So hot. You fit like a glove around me." He let his hands move from her shoulders down her back and up again while he continued to ravish her mouth with his tongue and lips. The taste of her was intoxicating. He couldn't get enough even if he kissed her forever.

The ache began at the base of his spine heating his balls until they were on fire with the need to come. "You there?" He slipped a finger down the crack of her ass until he could reach her back hole. "Please tell me you're there."

"Almost… I just need a little more."

He pressed his finger to her puckered little hole, pushing the digit inside to the first knuckle.

She shot off like a rocket, screaming his name, drawing his own climax from so deep he wasn't sure he'd ever recover.

Her head rested on his shoulder as their breathing and heart rates returned to normal.

"I should move, but not sure if my legs will work."

He gently laid her back on the bed, his softening cock slipping from inside her. "I need to go get rid of this. I'll be right back."

When he returned a moment later she curled up on her side his pillow resting under her cheek. Her gaze fixed on his face as a little wrinkle appeared between her eyebrows. "Something wrong?"

She shook her head, pushing her hair out of her face before she sat up. "I, uh need to get cleaned up." Her feet hit the floor for a second before she disappeared into the bathroom.

After he slipped on a pair of jeans, he sat on the side of the bed wondering where they went from here. She'd only be here a couple of weeks and then she'd be gone back to her life. Complications like her were the reason he didn't do relationships.

* * * *

Tori leaned her hands on the countertop of the bathroom staring at herself in the mirror. *What the hell was I thinking? I should never have let that happen.* Making love with Noah King was what fantasies were made of. But where did they go from here?

"Tori? Are you okay?"

"Yeah, I'm fine. I'll be out in a second." The clean clothes she brought before her shower still sat on the countertop. After she took a moment to wash up her lady parts, she slipped on her blouse and jeans. She wouldn't make a big deal of what happened. He wouldn't want that. Rock stars didn't do that kind of thing. Play it cool and let him drive this bus.

Plastering a smile on her lips, she opened the door to his bedroom to find him fully dressed and standing with both of his hands buried in his front pockets. She'd come to realize that was his typical self-preservation stance. "I thought we'd run back into town. I can show you where we used to practice when we were in high school. It's not much. Just an old warehouse with awesome acoustics. The band owns the building now, and we use it as a practice studio when we're in town."

"Sounds awesome. Can I take some pictures?"

"Sure."

They rode in silence for several moments before they pulled up in front of what appeared to be an abandoned building. "This is it?"

His lips lifted in a smile. "Yep. It doesn't look like much, but the inside is fantastic. We have state-of-the-art recording equipment already set up as well as the sound booth so we can record here if we want to. The record company has their way of doing things, of course, but I find I can lose myself in the sounds easier here than anywhere else."

The huge bay doors slid easily to the side once Noah had them unlocked. "I asked the guys to meet us here. I know we're on a break, except there's never a break in the music business. We're always writing music, writing lyrics, doing photo shoots, promoting, engaging on social media, or thinking about all those things."

"Sounds like a lot of work." Her heels clicked on the concrete floor as he moved toward the back of the building to what looked like something out of an industrial horror flick.

Chains, pulleys, and a large door stood before them when he stopped and grinned over his shoulder. "Welcome to the back lot of Iron Rogue. You can take pictures, but you must swear to never reveal the location of the studio, no matter what. This is our sanctuary and if our fans knew where it was, we would never get any peace, making it that much harder to produce music."

"I won't. I promise," she whispered, in awe that he would share something so personal with her.

As they stepped through the door she was greeted by a large open room. She wasn't sure what she expected although this seemed almost disappointing. No lights, no fanfare, even though there was a stage set up off to the left including a microphone for Noah, electric guitar for Alex, bass guitar for Aiden, and a drum set for Dylan.

She jumped at the sound of footsteps behind her a moment before the rest of the band appeared. Each band member wore jeans, t-shirts, and tennis shoes. The effect was magnificent and at the same time, sweet and simply normal.

"Are you sure it's a good idea to show her this, Noah?" Alex grinned as he walked past her and disappeared into the sound booth.

Next came Aiden and Dylan who took their spots next to their instruments. Aiden began tuning his guitar while Dylan tapped out a rhythm on the drums.

Noah stepped to the microphone doing what she considered was a sound check while Alex played with some buttons and knobs in the booth. "Tori, you should go to the sound booth. Alex, are there any tryouts today?"

"No, but we do have five tomorrow."

Tryouts?

"Five? Jesus, we'll be here all day tomorrow."

"You got something better to do?"

Noah's gaze connected with hers as a little smile formed on his lips. "Maybe."

Unsure of what that meant, Tori let herself hope he might want to continue with what happened earlier and maybe even see where this might go. She didn't want to hope, but her heart had other ideas.

"I'm here." An older gentleman with a substantial belly and a balding head appeared beside her a moment later. "Well, hello there. Who might you be?"

"I'm Tori. I'm here with the band."

"Well, sweetie, I assumed that." He disappeared inside the sound booth with Alex reappearing moments later and taking his place on the makeshift stage.

The older man's voice boomed over the speakers. "All right guys, let's see what you got. Something new? Something old? Let's rock it."

Tori scooted her butt up on the stool she noticed sitting against the wall, ready to see and hear what no one else had ever been exposed to, Iron Rogue *raw*.

She watched in awe as the guys went through some songs, most if not all she already knew. To see them unplugged was a treat any fan would love. Snapping off a few pictures, she tapped out some notes on her cell phone to keep track of what she was experiencing. The sights, the sounds, the smell…every emotion and every sense was engaged in watching the band like this. This would make some great stuff for the article.

"Hey, guys, I have something I want to run by you," Noah said. "It's some lyrics I've been working on."

"New material?" Alex questioned. "That's awesome."

"Yeah."

Tori sat up straighter, waiting to hear what Noah had written. The acappella version of the lyrics coming from his mouth sent goosebumps across her flesh. They were so soulful, she wished she'd been around during the emotions that caused the words. He sang from the heart, putting everything into the lyrics.

"Okay. Okay, I got this." Alex strummed a few chords on his guitar, picking out the melody of something fantastic. The rest of the band picked up their piece as if this song had already been written and they'd been playing it for years. It was awesome to see how in sync the guys were with each other. No wonder they were the best.

She hoped their buddy in the sound booth was getting this all down.

As the last chords drifted off into silence, Tori felt a tear slipped down her cheek. Her heart beat wildly in her chest as she tried to bring all of her emotions under control. The picture in her mind was of their fans the very first time they would hear the new song live. The quietness of the stadium would be deafening before they erupted into the loudest cheering she would ever hear. She hoped to God she would be around to see it.

By the end of the afternoon, she was wiped. Every emotion she could ever have imagined had whipped through her body several times while she listened. Watching Noah pour his heart and soul into every note and every lyric was something she would never forget. She'd seen him live several times, but this was something on a different level, something she wished his fans could see. Other than the pictures she'd taken, they never would.

They drove back to his house without a single word passing between them. She wished she knew what to expect. Did they go on acting as if earlier had never happened?

"The guys want to meet at the bar in town in a little while. You up for that?"

"Sounds like fun. Dinner and music?"

"Yeah, wear something sexy. I want to show you off." He pushed open the car door and stepped out arriving at her side in seconds only to open the door for her.

He wants to show me off? I'm not sure how to take that.

With his warm hand at the base of her spine, he guided her to the front door, unlocked it, and pushed it open. "After you."

She put her tote bag, which she carried everything in, on the kitchen island before heading to her room to change. Wear something sexy he said. Sexy? What the hell does that even mean? Yes, he'd made sure she had a knockout little black dress when they bought her clothes along with some strappy black shoes to wear with it. Unsure of how long they had before they were supposed to meet the guys, she hurried to get dressed, spritzing on some perfume before sliding the soft material over her curves. She did like the way she looked when she twisted back and forth in front of the mirror. It did make her look sexy. A little bit of makeup, a twist of her hair at the crown, and she was ready. Hopefully, she didn't look like she was trying to too hard.

When she arrived back in the living room a short time later, the look in his eyes when he turned and saw her made every insecurity about her appearance disappear. He obviously liked what he saw.

"You look gorgeous." He leaned in and pressed a soft kiss to her lips. "Shall we go?"

It took thirty minutes to arrive at the restaurant, and she spent every moment sneaking glances at Noah the whole time. He'd put on a nice white dress shirt and a pair of slacks with some gorgeous black boots on his feet. Rock star to gentleman in the blink of an eye. She was totally captivated.

The instant he stopped the car she felt so far out of her league she wasn't sure what to do. A canopy enclosed the carpeted walkway to the double wood and glass doors. The restaurant looked very exclusive and very expensive. A man stood on each side of the doors, dressed in tuxedos waiting to hold them open for the patrons. *Holy shit.*

One of the gentlemen opened the door, holding it for her while Noah came around and held out his hand to help her from the car. He tucked her hand in the crook of his arm leading her toward the doors as the two men swept them open.

"Good evening Mr. King. I believe your table is ready."

"Thank you."

They disappeared inside the building and Tori almost tripped over her feet as she took in the décor. Crystal chandeliers hung from the ceiling, the light from behind the crystals bouncing off the walls in a myriad of dancing color. Dark wood accented the marble on the walls, framing everything in a rich, wood. White tablecloths and real silver silverware graced every table, right along with real crystal goblets at each place setting.

"Right this way, Sir."

Tori had never been in a restaurant this fancy.

"Relax," Noah whispered next to her ear. "I'm right here."

The maître d' seated them at a private corner table where anyone else in the restaurant would be hard-pressed to see them.

Noah ordered some fancy wine she'd never heard of and grinned over the menu as she glanced down at the food selections, her stomach in knots. She wasn't sure she'd even be able to eat.

"Where are the rest of the guys?" she asked, glancing around them.

He took a sip of his wine, placing the glass back on the table near his fingers. "We're meeting them later. I wanted you to myself for a little while."

"Wow." She looked back at the menu, unsure of what to order. "I'm not even sure what half of the stuff is."

"The cheeseburgers are really good."

She glanced over the top of her menu not sure if she'd heard correctly. The grin on his face was infectious. "Cheeseburger?"

"Yep. That's what I get when I come here."

"Seriously?" She giggled but then pressed her fingers to her lips to stifle the sound. This place was much too fancy to be laughing at their dinner selections, but she just couldn't help it.

The waiter arrived a moment later to take their order. "My usual, please. Cheeseburger, no tomato and no onion."

"Of course, Mr. King." He glanced at Tori. "And for you, ma'am?"

She couldn't help but smile. "I'll have the same, only just no onion, tomato is fine."

"Very good." The waiter disappeared, leaving her and Noah alone.

After a sip of her wine, she glanced around, taking in the atmosphere of the place when really she didn't want to stare. Opulence abounded with each glass, each piece of cutlery, and each waiter who walked past.

Noah leaned back in his seat, sipping from his glass. One thing she'd noticed since they'd been home, he hadn't drunk whiskey even once. Rumor had it, he was an alcoholic. She hadn't seen anything to indicate that since she'd come home with him. "Can I ask you a question and you won't get offended?"

"Sure."

"It's been written that you have an alcohol problem, and I saw you drinking at the concert before we came here."

His brow furrowed as he set his glass down, his eyes going cold and distant. "I don't have a drinking problem."

Reaching across the table, she touched his fingers wanting to assure him of her allegiance, if anything. She didn't know what to believe. "I didn't say you did. I was asking because I hadn't seen you drink, except tonight, since we've been here in Iowa."

"I drink. I'll admit that." His gaze focused on his wine glass, shifting to her fingers for a moment before lifting to meet hers again. "You have no idea what it's like on the road, Tori. Night after night we spend a couple of hours on stage. For me singing, for the rest of the guys pounding out chords of music. It's a lonely existence sometimes. Yes, women throw themselves at us on a nightly basis. Everyone wants a piece of us, always wanting to tap into what's hot this week. We are rarely in the same city two nights in a row. Unless we take time off, like we are right now, we rarely get a break. The only reason we got this break is because I insisted, knowing something was going on with my family. The venues were not happy that we canceled shows."

"I can't even imagine being in a different city every couple of days." Sadness and understanding gripped her soul. His eyes looked lonely and unhappy.

He brought his wine glass to his lips, taking a sip before setting it back down. "I'm sure you've noticed none of us have a steady girl in our lives. How do you think she'd feel never having somewhere to call home? What about the women who constantly throw themselves at us? It would take one hell of a woman to tolerate the attention we receive."

Tori thought about how she would feel if she belonged to Noah. The constant touring, the never-ending women, the long nights and longer days, and the pressure of always needing to be on top would be like an open wound that never healed, festering until the fissure was so wide it could never be breached. "If you had it to do all over again, would you?"

He took a moment to think before he answered her question. "If I had it to do over again. If I take that in the context of our current conversation about the band, I would have to really think about that. But if you mean making love to you, I would in a heartbeat even if it's probably the worst thing I could do for both of us."

Their food arrived a second later, and while they ate, Tori contemplated their table talk. Had he meant what he said? Did he or didn't he want to make love to her again? She was so confused, she didn't know which way to turn and the bad part was, she didn't have anyone she could call to talk to about it because only Bella knew where she was, and her friend thought she should sleep with Noah as many times as she could. Anyone else would think she was crazy. How could she possibly explain she was in the middle of Iowa having dinner in a fancy restaurant with the sexy lead singer of the hottest band in the country? *Sure, Tori, and you've lost your ever-loving mind.*

Chapter Six

The next day found them back at the warehouse only this time there were several extra people, those vying for a spot she didn't know existed. It seemed Iron Rogue had decided to add a keyboardist.

Noah was focused on what was going on around him. The controlled chaos had him nervous and jumpy from what she could tell. He'd paced the floor several times, running his fingers through his hair absently, something she noticed he did frequently when he was stressed, like now.

Five hopeful keyboardists had gathered, waiting in the wings for their chance to impress the guys in the band. From what she knew it would take someone phenomenal to be able to impress the band and blend into their midst. There were four guys and one female. Tori was rooting for the woman even though she didn't like the thought of a girl in the band being around Noah all the time. The green vein of jealousy ran deep.

As each one did their best Tori couldn't tell who the guys liked, until Taylor stepped up to the keyboard. She couldn't have been more than five feet tall, with short blonde spiky hair and sporting a pink streak across the crown. She had the rocker look down to a "T" with her short-sleeved t-shirt, her skinny jeans, and the thin metal chain around her waist. Noah didn't look twice.

"All right, Taylor is it?" Noah said into the microphone.

"Yep, that's me." The girl grinned, her black lipstick a sharp contrast to her pale complexion.

"How long have you been playing?"

"Fifteen years."

"You can't be more than twenty."

"Twenty-five actually, but I've been playing since I was ten." She placed her hands on the keyboard. "What would you guys like to hear?"

"Do you know any of our songs?" Noah asked, his gaze shooting to Alex.

"I know all of them."

"All right. We're going to start with one, you come in and do your thing. We'll see how you blend."

The guys started one of their less popular songs and to Tori's amazement Taylor jumped right in and played along perfectly. Noah glanced at Alex, then it Aiden, and back at Dylan nodding with the slight tilt of his head as if to say yes. They played several more songs including Dare to Love. The addition of the keyboard on their most popular song made it that much better. Noah waved his hand halfway through the song, saying, "Whoa. Whoa. I think that's good."

Taylor stepped from behind the keyboard and moved toward the front of the stage. "Thanks for the chance, guys. This has been like a dream come true. Iron Rogue is one of my favorite bands, and I would love to have the opportunity to play with you guys all the time."

"Thanks, Taylor. We'll be in touch."

Taylor moved toward the doors glancing back and waving for a moment before she disappeared. Tori jumped to her feet, moving quickly toward Noah. "I have to say something. I know I'm not part of the band, but if you guys don't hire her, you're crazy. She was by far better than any of the rest."

Noah moved in front of her, running his fingers down her cheek for a second before he pressed a quick kiss to her lips, right in front of the rest of the band. "I have to agree with you."

When he stepped aside, she met the gazes of the rest of the guys, each one having the most comical expression on their face that she could ever imagine. Of course, none of them knew the extent of the relationship she and Noah shared, such as it was.

"Let's wrap it up," he said. "I'm beat."

Alex gave her a thumbs up. The others walked toward her, grinning like they had a secret, before moving on past to gather their stuff. Buddy came out of the sound booth. "That was fantastic guys. I got every bit recorded so you can go back and hear what transpired today although I have to say I agree with your lady friend, Noah. If you don't hire that girl, you're all crazy."

Tori grinned, silently hoping she wasn't being too bold to suggest anything. Her thoughts on the keyboardist didn't mean shit, but Noah seemed to take what she said into consideration. That meant a lot.

Once the lights were all off and they made their way toward the huge front doors, Tori began to wonder what tonight would bring. The few hours they'd spent with the guys at the bar after dinner, had been interesting. They'd shared stories, laughed, drank, and the whole time, Noah had stayed close. Not close enough to arouse suspicion with his bandmates, but close enough for her to realize he was there. His hand had rested on her thigh most of the evening, right at the edge of her dress while his fingers played with her bare skin. Wetness had coated the insides of her thighs, so much so she'd been afraid the back of her dress had been wet when they left. After their date not-a-date last night, they'd went their separate ways and slept alone. Noah had kissed her good night, a passionate melt your panties kiss that definitely made her realize he wanted her, but apparently wanting her wasn't enough to push him into sharing her bed. *The bastard.*

They pulled into the yard in front of the house and he turned off the car. Inky darkness surrounded them as the stars began to show in the night sky. She hadn't realized how late it had gotten until they'd stepped outside.

"Listen, Tori. I'm sorry about the other day."

"Sorry?"

"Yeah." He kicked a rock with his toe before glancing up at her. "Us getting physical probably isn't a good idea. You are only here for a few weeks and then you'll go back to your life."

"Noah." She put her hand on his forearm, stepping close enough to take in his scent. "I wanted to make love with you, and I'm a big girl. I can take care of myself, and I'm fully aware of the consequences of what we did. It was sex, nothing more, and I'm okay with that, really. I don't like the idea of being a notch on your bedpost, but at this point as long as we are both being adults, we should be able to handle whatever happens between us like adults." She tucked her heart away, brushed a kiss against his lips, and walked up the stairs of the house. Knowing the door was unlocked, she headed inside. Noah King would be a memory she could hold close, but in the end, he was not worth her tears…*not yet*.

The kiss at her bedroom door was not something she would forget even if he'd said nothing more, just simply went to his room, leaving her standing in the hall.

She flicked off the bathroom light a little while later as she got ready for bed. The notes on the session today needed to be typed up for her article. She had almost everything or thought she did, to make it a kick-ass write up on the guys. Of course, she'd agreed they'd all get a chance to read it before she sent it into her publisher. A few more tidbits and it would knock the socks off every rock fan in the industry. She sat down at the desk a moment later, adding a few more things she'd forgotten about today. The way everything had come together, seemed magical. She wished she could sit and watch a whole album be recorded from start to finish. That would be a memory for the books.

A soft knock on the bedroom door brought her head around to stare at it for a moment.

"Tori?"

"Yes?"

"Can I come in?" he asked, a slight uncertainty in his voice.

"Uh, sure."

As the portal opened, her breath caught. Noah stood in her doorway with nothing on but low-slung jeans. His chest glistened with water fresh from the shower she'd heard a few moments ago. Her belly began a low hum of excitement, traveling to her pussy as he took his time coming toward her. Her fingers tugged at the hem of her t-shirt, the one he'd given her the first night of their arrival. She'd slept in it every night just so she could smell his scent. "Is there something you needed?"

His eyes held hunger, dark and needy. "You."

He swept her up in his arms, bringing her chest to chest in front of him before his mouth crashed down on hers, devouring it in a kiss meant to stop any protest. Not that she would if her life depended on it.

Her head tilted as he skimmed his mouth along her cheek to her neck, nipping and sucking the skin. The whimper she heard came from somewhere deep inside her chest as her hands clutched at his shoulders in a vain attempt to hold him closer. She wanted to crawl inside his skin to feel everything he had to offer.

His hands disappeared beneath the shirt, pushing it up until she had no choice but to slip it over her head. His gaze fixed on her bare breasts before moving to her face. "You are absolutely the most beautiful thing I have ever seen in my life."

Knowing that probably wasn't the whole truth, she didn't care. It came from his mouth so she would tuck it into her memories.

He cupped her breasts, bending his head to take the right nipple into his mouth as his thumb caressed the left. She pushed her hips into his, feeling his rock hard erection against her belly. The low hum became a full on melody. His low moan of appreciation vibrated along her skin.

She tangled her hands in his hair, holding his head to her chest. The soft scratch of his facial hair abraded her skin enough to raise goosebumps. Her lips parted on a groan of restlessness. She needed more of him.

When she reached for the button at his waist, he raised his head, focusing on her face. His eyes were questioning. He was giving her the option of stopping this now or letting it take them to a place where only the two of them existed. Paradise awaited.

She unbuttoned his jeans, pushing them off his hips and down to his ankles. His erection looked hard and painful with veins snaking up the sides and the head purple and glistening with pre-cum. She wrapped her hand around his girth before sliding to her knees. He moaned as she took the head between her lips, letting it slide along her tongue.

"God, Tori."

This was for him.

Her hand began working his shaft as she slipped her mouth up and down his cock so no part was untouched. He fisted his hands in her hair guiding her to what he liked. His hips shifted toward her with every pass, increasing in speed until his hands were so tight on her scalp, it was painful. His breathing hitched for a second before he shuddered, shooting hot cum down her throat. The salty taste was the essence of Noah, and she wanted it all.

When she climbed to her feet, he kissed her on the lips even knowing his taste still lingered. "You didn't have to do that."

"I know. I wanted to," she whispered, touching the hair on his chin. "Are you sure about this?"

"I can't seem to stay away from you no matter how hard I try."

A little thrill went through her heart. Maybe he did care just a little.

He slipped his fingers over her cheeks before burying them in her hair at the base of her neck. His lips descended, touching hers in a soft brush. After a few nips, he dove in, taking her mouth in a punishing, demanding crashing of lips. His tongue thrust, sparring with hers back and forth until she couldn't breathe.

Need grip her like a fist, settling low in her belly until she thought she'd scream. "Noah, please."

Free from his jeans, he pushed her shorts down over her hips before walking her backward toward the bed. She took a seat on the edge before she started to shift toward the middle.

"Uh-uh," he said, pulling her hips back to the edge.

Nudging her legs apart, he went down on his knees, burying his face between her thighs before she could take her next breath. The brush of his tongue on her clit sent tingles straight to her spine, driving a deep needy moan from her lips. He nipped at the insides of her thighs before soothing the sting with his tongue. Each swipe forced whimpers of desire from her mouth, urging him on for more. Good grief the man had a talented tongue. The moment he pushed two fingers into her, she couldn't hold back her orgasm any more than she could finish a sentence. Stars exploded behind her eyelids as she cried out his name.

As she came down from her high and her breathing slowed, he kissed the insides of her thighs then came to his feet. He reached for his pants, removing a condom from the front pocket.

"Hopeful or cocky?"

"Wishful?" His eyebrows drew together as he frowned. "I don't know what this is between us, Tori, but you—I can't seem to think beyond being inside you, but if this isn't what you want, say so now."

"I want, Noah, more than you'll ever know." He searched her eyes for a moment and then rolled the condom down his cock. With a hand on each leg, he spread her open for him and stepped between them, lining himself up with her pussy. The head of his cock pushed inside her, drawing a greedy groan from her mouth. "Yes. That's it. Give me all of you."

The fullness, the absolute beauty of being one with this man brought tears to her eyes, but she blinked them away. Getting emotional would be a moment killer at this point. She'd worried about those feelings when she was alone in her bed later and could examine them to her heart's contentment. Right now, the man above her in all his magnificence needed to fill her until she had nothing else to give.

Once he was fully seated inside her, she shifted her hips slightly to ease the discomfort. He wasn't a small man in the length department, but she wouldn't have it any other way.

"You okay?"

"Oh, hell yes. I'm perfect or will be as soon as you start moving."

He closed his eyes as if he was fighting for control before he began a slow glide. A shudder shook him for a second. His cock moved in and out of her pussy like he had nowhere else to be. His jaw ticked as if he ground his teeth to keep his own orgasm at bay.

She reached up, touching her fingertip to his nipple, rubbing it slightly as he hissed.

"You're killing me." His gaze seared her with its heat, scorching her skin where it touched.

"Good. Join the party."

He slammed into her, rendering her breathless as he began to pound into her. The fierceness of his taking branded her with his essence, his need, and the fiber of his being. She would never be the same again.

His lips descended, taking her mouth in a possessive kiss. His tongue pushed past her lips, tangling with hers. "All that wetness for me," he whispered, pressing his forehead against hers.

His hips did a little grinding motion as he continued his thrusting, pushing his pelvis against her clit, but the moment he rubbed his finger right over the top of the hard nub, her orgasm rolled over her like a wave. "Noah!"

"Fuck yes. That's it. Give me everything," he growled, taking his own pleasure as she continued to ride the high.

The moment his orgasm began to fade, he rested his head against her shoulder, his breath hot on her skin. The closeness brought it all home. She wanted more.

* * * *

Two days later found him and Tori standing in his parents' living room with every one of his siblings close at hand. All of them had given him a side-long look when he'd introduced them, which he couldn't blame them. He'd never brought a woman home before, and he wasn't sure how to explain her presence or what was going on between them. The whole situation had him on edge.

"All right. Now that you're all here, we can get down to why your mother and I called you all home," his father said, taking a seat near the fireplace in his favorite recliner. "For a while now, I haven't felt well. I won't go into details as I'm sure you would all be bored with it, but several weeks ago, I went to the doctor. I had noticed things I hadn't before. Pain in my belly, unable to breathe very well at certain times, itching all over, things like that seemed to be happening more and more."

"Dad, what's going on?" Noah asked.

His father glanced from one child to another. "I'm dying."

"What?"

"What the hell are you talking about?"

"Daddy?"

Every one of his children spoke at the same time until he held up his hand to silence them all. "It's okay. I've talked to the doctors, along with your mother. They've done test after test and it appears I have liver cancer that has spread to my lungs or vice versa. I'm not sure which."

"We'll get it treated. You know I can afford to have whatever done that needs to be done, Dad. We'll see specialists, bring in the best doctors—" he said, moving to his father's side and taking his hand. "We won't give up."

"Noah, son, it's done. The doctors said there is nothing more they can do. I've let it go on too long without treatment."

"There has to be something."

"There isn't."

Sophia and Mia cried silently on the couch, each clutching the others hand as tears streaked down their cheeks. Ben now stood by the window looking out over the front of the house, deep in his own thoughts. Elijah and Daniel stood side-by-side, unsure of what to do or say as they looked at him for what to do. Noah was just as lost as they were.

"I have chosen not to try anything to make this better, my children. I've lived a good life. Your mother and I have been happy for a lot of years and I have set her up so she can stay here, on our property, until the day she dies and joins me in heaven. We've prepared everything we can for when the time comes, but you all need to know there is nothing for you to do here. We will function as normal until the time I can no longer do that. I have hired a foreman to take over the ranch, someone I trust, that way they will be in place when everything is said and done. When your mother goes to meet the Lord along with me, the property will be sold and divided amongst you all since I know none of you wish to run this place full time." His father struggled to stand before bringing his children in close. "I love you all, you know that, but this is my choice and I don't want to deal with all the pain, sickness, and everything that goes along with chemotherapy and all that. I just want to die in my home as pain-free as possible. Can you all do that for me?"

Noah's gaze moved to Tori's face. Her sad eyes held his for a moment before he looked away. He would do what needed to be done for his family. "We will abide by your wishes, Dad. We love you."

His dad touched his cheek. "I know, Noah. You are my eldest, and I know you'll help me through this as much as you can, but none of you will give up your lives to be here. Your mother and I can handle this until such time, but we'll let you know."

"But—"

"No buts, son. You are home on a hiatus for now, but you will not give up the band for me. I will not have it."

He would have to do as his father asked, although, since they would be home for a while yet, he was going to do whatever he could to help. He'd be damned if his father would have to lift a finger if he didn't want to.

The afternoon wore on with whispers of comfort and tears all the way around. Noah's steps took him out the back screen door of the kitchen, onto the patio overlooking the pasture. Sun beat down on his head and shoulders as he thought about what they'd learned today. Cancer. *Fuck.* He wasn't sure how to even take this news. His father was everything to him, the man he'd grown up looking to for advice on women, work, the band, marketing, and life. He always knew they would be gone someday, but someday was coming on faster than he was prepared for.

Arms went around his waist from behind and a cheek rested on his shoulder. "You okay?"

He shrugged, unsure what else to do at this point. Tori kissed his shoulder and laid her head back down.

"If you need to talk, I'm here."

"I know. Thanks."

"He's a strong man."

"Yes, he is, the strongest I've ever known."

She slipped her arms from around his waist, but before she could disappear he turned to face her. Standing tough in front of him was a woman he'd come to care for more than he could say. He didn't know how to handle everything going on around him. It was too much. He needed a drink or sex or both.

"Let's go." He grabbed her hand and headed for the car.

"Now? Are you sure?"

"Yeah. I need you."

Dragging her behind him, he reached the car, almost shoving her inside before he took off in a spray of gravel down the driveway. He knew his siblings would be pissed, but he didn't care. He had to handle this his own way, and his way was to bury himself inside the sweet heat of the woman he had staying with him.

The moment they hit the hardwood in his house, he had Tori's pants down around her left ankle, her panties pushed aside, and his cock free from his pants. Lifting her so she straddled his hips, he backed her against the front door, slamming his cock up inside her to the hilt. "Fuck."

"Yes, that's it, Noah. Use me. I know you need this."

"You have no idea."

"I do. Fuck me hard."

She bit his neck where the muscle and his shoulder met, forcing him to almost blow his load in one swift thrust, but he managed to push it back down at the last minute. She needed to come too, and he'd be damned if he would be the only one enjoying this.

He slipped his cock from her heat and dragged her over the couch, pushing her down on her belly over the arm. With her ass high in the air, he shoved his cock back into her hot, tight pussy, pulling a deep groan from his chest. She was the tightest and sweetest woman he'd ever known.

Each thrust of his hips drove a cry of pleasure from her mouth until she was panting yes, yes, yes with every slam of his pelvis.

His balls drew up against his groin signaling the end of this ride as he felt heat gathering at the base of his spine. He couldn't blow without taking her along for the ride. "Lift your hips a little."

When she did, he slipped a finger around to her front and began rubbing her clit in quick, bold strokes meant to bring her to orgasm quickly. Her pussy tightened around him, pulling his own orgasm to the front until he could no longer hold back.

Her high scream echoed off the walls as he pumped his hips, dragging his orgasm out until he felt like he couldn't move. *What have I done?*

Chapter Seven

Noah pulled his softening cock from her body before jerking up his pants. "Shit. I'm sorry, Tori. I shouldn't have done that."

She slowly rose, dragging up her jeans over her hips and buttoning them at the waist. Once she'd located her t-shirt and pulled it on, she shoved her fingers through her hair trying to straighten it a little. "Nothing to be sorry for. You had a need. I fulfilled it. We're good." She rose up on her toes and kissed him on the lips. "Shall we get some food?"

Flabbergasted at her casual attitude toward him using her body like that, he stared for a moment before following her back out to his car. She jabbered all the way back to town, although he really hadn't been listening until she mentioned their upcoming tour dates.

"Uh, I'm not sure where the first stop is. I've kind of lost track."

"How much longer are you guys on this forced break?" she asked, even though her gaze was fixed out the window when he looked.

"Two months, give or take." He turned down the main road in town, heading out the other side.

She turned in the seat so she faced him a little. Her eyes were bright and curious with questions, but unrevealing to him as to whether she was upset by what happened earlier. "I don't know if I told you, but the new song you wrote is fantastic. Your fans are going to love it."

"I'm not so sure of that. They like the hard stuff and it's a ballad. They are more into the raw songs, rough and strong in their beat."

"True, but I'm sure you have something that will blow the speakers inside you somewhere too." Her grin reached her eyes, making him realize he had no idea what went on in her brain, but he really liked the way her face lit up when she smiled.

"You're good for my ego."

"Just stating the truth. You are an awesome lyrist. You can write words like a poet and make people feel emotions they didn't know they had in them."

He kept driving, not really knowing where he wanted to take her, only someplace away from Sommerton. They'd spent the last week there, and he really hadn't shown her much of the area. They only had seven more days before he had to let her go.

"Where are we going? I don't recognize this area."

The radio played a song he knew from another band he liked. The rhythm was something he could get into. It fit right into his mood, something questioning, something that made him think beyond his own wants and needs for a change. "I thought we go to the next town over to eat. They have a great Chinese restaurant. I hope you like Chinese. It's quite a bit bigger in size than Sommerton."

She didn't say anything for a moment, making him wonder what was going through her mind.

"Sounds good."

The car pulled up in front of the restaurant where a small crowd had gathered in front of the doors. He wondered who was here that would cause such a commotion. The crowd parted as he walked Tori toward the door with his hand at the small of her back. Hoping no one noticed them, he walked with his head down, attempting to curtain his face with his hair.

A high-pitched scream of his name brought his head around as a young, leggy blonde launched herself into his arms, effectively pushing Tori to the side.

"Oh my God, it's Noah King!"

The woman draped herself over his chest, wrapping her arms around his neck. His hands automatically went to her hips. He had no idea who she was, except she was apparently a fan.

"I didn't realize you were in town. I absolutely love all of your music. You are my favorite rock star." She brought her lips next to his ear. "My apartment is close, if you know what I mean."

Noah pulled her arms from around his neck. "Uh, thanks for the invite but I'm here with someone." He stood there for a moment, taking pictures with several of the women with the blonde. He had to do his part for the band. It was all in being a rock star.

Tori stood off to the side with her arms crossed over her chest and a frown on her face. He couldn't blame her. This was his life. This was his existence. This was the reason he didn't have a steady girl. Most couldn't handle this. He couldn't help if she was furious.

Once they disappeared through the double doors he could relax a little. Hopefully, they would seat them quickly, so they could leave the groupies outside behind. "I'm sorry about that."

"Does that happen a lot?"

"Yes, actually. More often than I like. It doesn't happen a lot in Sommerton because we grew up there. In the different cities we travel to, it happens everywhere."

They took their seats at the table, waiting for the waiter to arrive. He liked this particular restaurant simply for the atmosphere. It was usually calming, tonight, not so much. Being accosted outside had left a bad taste in his mouth.

"I can see were having women throw themselves at you all the time would be frustrating. Just out of curiosity, how many nights have you actually not been with a woman? Can you even tell me?" Her left eyebrow shot up over her eye.

Noah had to think about it for a moment before he answered. Lately, the nightly rotating carousel of groupies had been tiring even before they came home. He couldn't come up with a number for her. There wasn't any way of knowing.

"Do you even know the name of the last woman you slept with?"

He grinned with a little mischievous smile. "Yeah. Tori."

Her look said *do I look stupid*.

A fuzzy picture formed in his brain of two nights before he met Tori. The girl was brunette, if he remembered right. She'd been slim, sporting several tattoos along her arms. Her name? He had no fucking clue. "I couldn't tell you."

"I could've guessed."

"Doesn't really matter?" His hand slid over the top of hers where it rested on the table. "This is part of my life, Tori. Being recognized everywhere we go can be trying."

"And the women?" she asked, sliding her hand out from under his.

He thought about how to answer. She already knew the truth. She probably knew more about him than a lot of people. "They come and they go. An endless sea of faces, we rarely see twice. They all blend together after a while."

After a moment or two, she posed another question. "Have you ever been in love?"

"Truthfully?"

"Yes."

The last thing he needed was this splashed across the pages of Rock Band News. "Are you asking as a reporter?"

It took her a moment to answer, but when she did, the look in her eyes told him she was serious. "No. I'm asking as me."

What does that mean? He knew he cared about her more than he should. How could he not? Her heart was simple but golden in its light. He saw the way she cared as her eyes grew sad when they'd heard the news from his dad. She didn't really know him or his family. She'd still offered comfort in a time where he needed someone, and that someone had been her. "I'm not sure that I have."

"You don't know if you've been in love?" Her eyes told him she didn't believe him.

"I don't think I've ever felt that all-consuming need to be with one person for the rest of my life. Don't get me wrong, Tori, I want that. I want what my parents have. To wake up next to the same person day after day and not get bored? I'm not sure I have it in me." Having spent the last seven days with Tori was probably the closest thing he'd ever come to being with someone on a long-term basis. They'd eaten together, showered together, made love, and spent time getting to know each other. She'd seen more of the real man than any other person since the band got started.

Her eyes clouded with seriousness as she contemplated what he said. He could almost see the thoughts dancing through her mind.

When the food arrived, they ate in silence. He didn't want to screw up the rest of their time together. He'd begun to look forward to spending his days being nothing more than Noah King, the man rather than Noah King the rock star. He kind of liked how she'd taken over the bathroom, how she sang off key in the shower, how she'd begun to cook for the two of them without being asked, and the way they'd talked, really talked about things like life. He didn't dare put a name to anything going on between them. He couldn't.

* * * *

Tori walked up to Alex's house, glancing backward as Noah watched her from his truck near the curb. She needed to do interviews with each of the guys for her article so she could learn a little more about the rest of the band instead of just Noah. This was her chance to get the goods on Alex, Aiden, and Dylan, each in their own environment. It took a bit of convincing to get Noah to leave her and let her do this on her own. He didn't seem too keen on the idea of her talking to the guys without him there.

She turned back toward the front door and rung the bell. Within a moment or two, Alex pulled open the door, swept her up in a hug, and then waved at Noah before shutting it behind them.

"You did that to piss him off, didn't you?"

"Yep." His lips lifting in a teasing grin. "Believe it or not, Tori, you've gotten to him. I have never seen him this possessive over anyone."

A sweep of the room revealed a surprisingly comfortable space. "I don't believe it, but it's nice of you to say." Big fluffy looking couches spread along the wall to her right, taking up the entire space. The room was huge with high ceilings, dark wood beams running lengthwise, white walls, gorgeous hardwood floors, and bright colored pillows tossed about. To her left stood a large archway that led into a kitchen any chef would be proud of. Black cabinets accentuated the white marble countertops and the white subway tile backsplash. The appliances were top of the line black with matte finishes. "Wow. Holy hell, Alex. This is gorgeous."

"Thanks." He took her hand in his and led her down the hall. "Let's go in here," he said, pushing open the door, revealing an office space with a huge mahogany desk, a couple of file cabinets, and a wide bay window overlooking his back lawn.

She stepped up to the window, glancing out at the manicured space. "Do you do your own gardening?" Green lawn stretched as far as she could see, but right in the center was a gorgeous flower garden with large shrubs, several different flowers species, and a beautiful fountain where the water burbled loud enough she could hear it inside the house.

"No. We aren't home enough to keep it like that. I would kill everything if I tried, although I do some when we are here."

Making a mental note to add that to her article, she looked a little further out, noting there was a small lake with a dock and a boat. "You have a boat?"

"Yeah. It's not much. It is something to row out onto the water when it gets hot in the summer. I like to fish out there too. I have it stocked with a few different kinds of fish to keep it interesting."

Another tidbit. When she turned back to face him, she was struck by his looks. If she wasn't so taken with Noah, she'd think he was really hot with his long blond hair, blue eyes, and killer smile. Something lurched behind his eyes though. Something she couldn't quite put her finger on it. He was taller than Aiden and Dylan, but not quite as tall as Noah. His chest was broad and his biceps were toned along with his abs from what she remembered from one of their photoshoots where all the guys had their shirts open. At this moment, he wore a form-fitting T-shirt and low-slung jeans with bare feet, the ultimate relaxed rock star.

"Why don't we sit here," he said, showing her two chairs sitting cattycorner from each other. "That way we can talk and I can still see your pretty face."

Heat infused her cheeks as she glanced at the floor. Flirting was Alex's forte, not something she was really comfortable with. She needed to get used to it though since this was Alex in all his glory.

"So. What would you like to know about Alex Rockly that no other woman knows?"

She pulled out a small notebook, one she'd been writing her information in for the article and wrote Alex across the top. The first several pages were notes on Noah, some things she wouldn't reveal to anyone. "Let's see. I need to ask a few things that are general to all of you and then we'll get personal."

One blond eyebrow rose as a sexy little grin lifted his lips. "I like personal."

"When you get a song idea, what is the first thing you do?"

Alex rubbed his fingers along his jaw, leaving a scraping sound behind as his eyes focused on something on the wall. "I usually run it over in my head several times, trying to decide if it sounds right before I put it to guitar and play it out. As you know, Noah and I write a lot together. He does lyrics and I do melody. I hear the music and he's good about putting the words to it. Sometimes he has the lyrics before I have the music, like with the new song we did the other day."

"I was blown away by how you guys pulled that together. It was fantastic to watch."

The sexy lift of his lips was back. "Thanks. It did work out great. It doesn't happen a lot."

She jotted down some notes in her book, flipping the pages as she tried to remember everything he said. "At what age did you first pick up a guitar?"

"I was eight. I played acoustic for a few years before I realized the fun in the electric guitar. You can do so much more with it."

"Did you always want to play in a band?"

Alex leaned in, placing his elbows on his knees as he clasped his hands together. "I guess I did, yes, the moment I realized chicks loved guys who played in a band."

This led right into some of the personal things she wanted for the article. "Have you ever been in love?"

"Nope. Too many chicks to pick from. I like variety. This week I may want a blonde, next week a brunette."

"Is there a particular type of woman who would catch your eye?"

"They all catch my eye, Tori, but if you mean is there a woman who would fit the description of someone I would fall in love with? I'm not sure. I like women with curves, not one who is afraid to eat if I take her out for a meal. I dig a girl who is a tiger in bed. If she's into a little kinky shit, then all the better."

He pulled his hair back off his shoulders, tying it in a band at the base of his neck. "I like to work out, so if she's into lifting weights, and running, then that's a plus. She can't be the jealous type. We have a lot of women throwing themselves at us all the time."

"Are you the type to go out with more than one woman at a time?"

"Go out?"

"You know…date?"

"I rarely date anyone. I don't have time. The band is my life which means there isn't space for anyone on a serious level." His eyes grew thoughtful for a moment. "I haven't met the one woman who could turn my world upside down. Am I looking? Not necessarily, but if she were to drop into my lap, then I would have to rethink everything that is my life, I guess."

"One last question." She was almost afraid to ask this one, it was so personal, but she wanted something that would shock the fans as well as making the guys human. "What is your favorite sexual position?"

Alex's eyes lit up with laughter. His gaze roamed over her face, her breasts, her waist, and then stopped before coming back to her eyes. "Favorite sexual position? Hmm. Well, I would have to say something that would give me access to the woman's most erogenous zones. Exploring her body to my hearts fill and giving her the best orgasm of her life is my ultimate fantasy. Hearing her scream my name as she comes is at the top of my list."

The temperature in the room rose twenty degrees, not because she was interested in Alex. The image flashing through her mind was of Noah bending her over the arm of the couch when he'd made her come so hard, she saw stars. Her body hummed with anticipation of seeing him again that night and every night until she had to go home. If he wanted to use her body for his pleasure, so be it. She would just have to guard her heart with everything inside her. Falling in love with Noah King was not a good idea.

Her next stop was Aiden's house. Noah had gone to his parents' for the afternoon while she did her errands, but Alex was more than willing to give her a lift over there. The house that belonged to Aiden's mother was a cute cottage style with big windows and a bright yellow front door. Flowers lined the walkway, blooming in various colors that made the whole house cheery.

Tori knocked on the door, expecting Aiden to answer.

"Hello. You must be Tori." Aiden's mother held out her hand. "I'm Elizabeth Rains, but please, call me Liz." Tori followed her inside as she shut the door behind them. "Aiden is down in his hole. Let me call him up. You can either follow him down there to see his space or you can talk up here. Either way is fine." His mother walked to a door at the end of the hall, opening it so she could yell down the stairs. "Aiden? Tori is here."

"I'll be right up."

Liz closed the door and waved Tori into the open kitchen. It wasn't very big, but the white cabinets and butcher-block countertops gave it a farmhouse feel. "Please, have a seat. Would you like tea, water, coffee, or something else?"

"Water would be great. Thank you."

"I also have some lemon bars I made if you'd like one."

"I would. Thanks again. Lemon bars are my favorite." Tori took a chair at the dining room table, sitting her notebook on the top. Her glance focused on Aiden's mother for a second, realizing how much her son favored her in appearance. Aiden had close-cropped hair, but he wore it longer on top. Its almost black color made his hazel eyes stand out even more. His mother had the same dark hair and gorgeous eyes, making her wonder about his father. From what she'd read, Aiden's dad took off when he was very young.

Aiden pushed open the door to what appeared to be steps going down as music floated up to reach her ears. She couldn't place the tune, although it sounded familiar.

"Hey."

"Hi. Thanks for meeting with me."

He slid into a chair across from her as his mother put down a glass of water and a plate with two lemon bars. "Can I get you something, Aiden?"

"Those look good and maybe a cup of coffee?"

"Sure, baby."

Aiden glanced at her notebook. "Are you getting lots of stuff for your article?"

"Some, yes." She took a bite of the dessert, letting it sit on her tongue for a moment as she savored the tart taste along with the sweetness of the powdered sugar. "These are fabulous."

"Thank you," Liz said, putting some down in front of Aiden. "They're his favorite too."

Tori wrote Aiden on the top of the next page and set down her pen. "I'm asking you guys a few general questions about the band and then moving onto a few personal questions."

"Sounds like a plan."

"If there is something you're not comfortable telling me, let me know, and I'll see if I can rephrase it so we don't have to give everything away." She glanced at his mother and then back to him.

"I'll go into the den and read for a bit. You let me know when you're done."

"Thanks, Mom."

"Let's see. You play bass in the band. Did you always want to play guitar?"

"No. I was into sports a lot when I was in high school. I picked up the guitar because I got hurt playing football. Broke my ankle."

"Ouch."

"Yeah." He leaned back in the chair, folding his hands over his abdomen.

Tori took a long look at her subject, formulating the questions she wanted to ask. "Do you do any of the songwriting?"

Aiden got a look in his eyes that Tori tried to decipher. He wasn't the shy one of the group, but he wasn't in your face like Alex either. He was cute in his own way, hot like the rest with his wide chest and almost nerdy look. The girl's seemed to really take to him, just like the others. "Not really. I will jump in with the bass when we jam, but that's about it. I'm not a lyrics guru like Noah, and Alex is the bomb on the electric."

She smiled as she wrote down his answers, thinking that he was being very modest from what she'd seen the other day. He'd been fantastic picking up the beat of the song none of them knew until that very moment. "You live here with your mom. Have you thought about getting your own place? Maybe settling down with a nice girl?"

His gaze fixed on the wall behind her for a moment as a small smile lifted the corners of his mouth. "I love my mom to pieces. When my dad took off, her and my sister were my everything. I can't imagine not being with them. Do I want a family of my own? Yeah, someday, but for now, I'm good right here when we're in town, which isn't a lot. Settling down?" He laughed, a rich dark laugh that made her smile. When he looked back at Tori, she could see something more in his eyes, a sadness or loneliness, she guessed, before he gave her his signature grin and said, "I hope I run into the right woman."

His answer gave her pause. Had he loved and lost someone in his past? "Have you ever been in love?"

"Yeah. Once. Things didn't work out."

"I'm sorry."

He shrugged his shoulders and fixed her with a stare. "It's okay. It wasn't meant to be, I guess. Bad timing and all that."

"Thanks, Aiden. I've got everything I need for now. If I think of something else, I'll let you know." She climbed to her feet and pulled out her cell phone to call a cab.

"Are you headed to Dylan's next?"

"Yes. He's the last one."

"I'll give you a lift. My mother wanted something from the store anyway, and he's on my way."

She leaned in and hugged him, hoping to take the look from his gaze, for a moment at least. "I would appreciate it. Noah drove me to Alex's, but he's being kind of surly today."

Aiden grinned and patted her shoulder. "Normal behavior for Noah most of the time."

He called out to his mother to let her know they were leaving before they walked out to his car. The classic mustang suited him to perfection. Red with white interior, the whole thing was tricked out with all the bells and whistles of a car from that era. She didn't even dare run her fingers over the fender.

"Wow. This is gorgeous."

His eyes held pride and love for the old car. "Thanks. One of my guilty pleasures, you could say. I bought it a long time ago and restored it to what it is now. I don't get to drive it as much as I would like." He ran his palm up the chrome beside the windshield, lovingly caressing the body of the car.

With the door held for her, she slipped inside, adoring the feel of the leather underneath her. The heat from the seat felt warm against her butt, almost scorching her skin. The sunshine on the white interior blinded her for a moment as Aiden slipped inside and turned over the engine. The low hum rattled along her nerves, calming her whole body with a slight purr. *Magnificent.*

Eyes turned as they rolled down main street Sommerton on their way to Dylan's. The attention was disconcerting to her, although it didn't seem to bother Aiden at all. She supposed he was used to it by now.

When they drove into Dylan's yard, the sight surprised her. Noah had mentioned Dylan liked his privacy, but this seemed extreme. You couldn't see the house from the road for all the old growth trees. "Wow. This is very private." The house wasn't anything fancy, more like an old cabin with roughhewn walls and a large wrap around porch.

"Dylan likes his privacy."

"I can see that."

Dylan walked out onto the porch and waved as Tori climbed from the car. "Hey, guys."

"Hi," she said, walking toward him as she took him in.

Dark hair framed his face, falling slightly into his eyes before he could push it back out of the way. Like Noah, he wore facial hair short along his jaw and framing his mouth, keeping it well trimmed and sexy. His dark eyes sparkled with laughter as he held out his hand to help her onto the porch.

"Welcome to my home."

"Thank you. It's really nice."

A deep rumble of laughter reached her ears. "Not what you'd expect from a rock star, eh?"

Her lips lifted in a smile. "Not really, no. It suits you though." Flowers were planted along the railing, giving the house a homey feel. White curtains blew in the breeze of the open windows, rustling softly. Birds jumped from tree limb to tree limb above the rooftop, chirping happily. A low hum of a tractor could be heard in the distance, and she glanced over to her right trying to find it. Nothing gave her any clue where the sound came from.

"I'll see you guys later. I think we are meeting at Rudy's tomorrow for drinks, right?"

"Yeah, I believe so," Dylan said as he led Tori to a seat on the porch. "Would you like something to drink?"

"That would be great, thank you. It's kind of warm today."

Aiden waved as he drove back down the long driveway and Dylan disappeared inside the house for a moment. When he returned a few seconds later, he held a glass of lemonade in his hand. "I hope lemonade is okay with you. I can get you some water if you prefer."

"No. This is perfect," she said, taking the glass and sipping the refreshing liquid. The tart taste smoothed out into something sweet as the coldness slipped down her throat. "Wonderful. You make a great host."

He took the rocker across from her, settling in with an ankle resting over the opposite knee. Decked out in a tight black t-shirt and a worn pair of jeans with black boots on his feet, he did not look like a rock star at all. His fingers were long and lean resting on his knee. A drummer's hands, she supposed. She could totally picture him holding his sticks and beating the hell out of his drum set as he rocked whatever song they were doing. Sweat would be streaking down his temple, his lips creased in a quirky smile, and his eyes sparkling in the stage lights as every girl in the stadium wished they would be his for the night.

"Tori?"

"Oh, yeah, sorry. I had a picture in my head that was intriguing."

"Oh?"

"Yeah, I bet you don't have any trouble getting women after the shows, do you?"

A blush snaked up his neck, turning the skin a crimson color. "Not like the other guys. The guy in the back is usually invisible."

"You are anything but invisible, Dylan."

"Thanks, I guess." He took a sip of his own lemonade before he spoke again. "So what kind of questions do you have for me?"

"How long have you been playing drums?"

"Since I was about six." A rumble of a laugh escaped his lips. "My parents bought them for me for Christmas, cursing the whole time as I beat the hell out of them."

She smiled thinking about a very young Dylan with his hair in his eyes, pounding out a rhythm only he knew. "How did you hook up with the others to join the band?"

"I knew Aiden from our hometown. I even dated his sister for a short time." A glance out over the pasture behind her gave her pause. Was there were more to the story? But when he focused on her again, his eyes had cleared of the memory. "Aiden knew I played drums, so he asked me to join them. We synced pretty well."

"You guys are awesome together. The other day when you all picked up Noah's new song and went with it, it was something I am glad I got to witness it."

"Thanks. That doesn't happen often. This time it worked."

"How does it feel to be the guy in the back?"

"Lonely."

The pause in his answer made her wonder what was going through his mind.

"Sometimes I wonder if people would even realize if I wasn't there." He looked down at the glass in his hand before bringing it to his lips again. "Sorry. I don't mean to be melodramatic. Noah's the lead singer. He is in your face with his personality. I love him like a brother, but sometimes I want to strangle him with the way he plays women and doesn't take things seriously. Alex is a front man too. He does his best to play off his need to be in front of everyone. He can't stand to be pushed to the back, but he gets bored easily. I wonder how long he'll be around. Aiden got hurt in the past. He plays it off, but I know he wants to find someone to settle down with. Our life doesn't make that easy."

Tori's brain was stuck on Noah and Dylan's words. She didn't want to be a plaything for Noah, although she couldn't shake the feeling she was nothing more than that. "Do you want to settle down eventually?"

The little quirky smile was back with a slight tilt to his lips. "Of course." He leaned in, setting his now empty glass on the ground beside his chair.

"Would you be against hooking up with someone in the industry or would you rather they be not connected to the music business at all?"

"You know, I hadn't really thought about it." He rubbed the whiskers on his chin for a moment before he smiled again. "It might be more convenient to have someone in the business. They would know all the ins and outs of the travel, the fans, the long hours, and the promotion."

"What about Taylor Valentine? The keyboardist who you guys saw the other day? She seemed really talented and spot on with you guys."

A red flush snaked up his neck as his gaze fixed on a spot over her shoulder. Tori knew she'd hit a spot with Dylan. He liked the girl.

"Bad idea to have a woman in the band, no matter how good she is."

"What if she hooked up with one of you, say Alex?"

"I'd have to kick his ass."

Chapter Eight

Thunder rumbled across the sky, rattling the windows of the old farmhouse as lightning streaked off in the distance. Noah stood at the window of his room watching the storm rage outside, battling with the thoughts in his head.

Tori slept peacefully in his bed, her head resting on the pillow he'd vacated when he'd gotten up over two hours ago. Their lovemaking had been off the charts, his body responding to hers like nothing he'd ever felt before. Heat simmered below the surface whenever they were in the same room, much less touching. He couldn't seem to keep his hands off her no matter what he tried. Kissing her was like breathing, he couldn't stop, didn't want to. His lips found hers every chance he got. His body sought hers whenever they got close, always skimming her arm with his fingers, brushing his lips over her shoulder, or running his hands through her hair.

The sheet rested at her waist, baring her breasts to his gaze. Her hand lay in the spot where his body had warmed the sheets, as if silently searching for him. A sigh escaped her lips, drawing his thoughts to the sounds she made when he filled her. Those sexy moans undid him.

Fuck. I'm in deep trouble here.

She understood him better than anyone he'd ever been with. The look in her eyes told him as much every time they came together. The clear emotions simmering there made him want things he couldn't have.

Bringing her here was a bad idea. He should have listened to his head when this all started, but he hadn't. He'd taken his interest in her to the logical conclusion of his past and ran with it, giving into the baser needs of his body before he realized she'd become more than just another woman in such a short time.

The complication of her drove him to push her away. He had to. She didn't need the problems he would bring to her life. The rock star bad boy didn't need her.

She would be in a couple of days. Better to cut and run now, before he got in any deeper.

With his pants and a T-shirt over his arm, he silently walked out the bedroom door and headed to the kitchen for coffee. The sun would be up soon, burning off the remaining storm, and making the rain glistening on the grass look like diamonds. The early mornings were his favorite time when he was home and today would be no different. He had work to do at the house.

Coffee gurgled in the pot as the last bits of water swished through the grounds. Noah had already grabbed a hearty cup from the dripping pot long before the last of the brew had finished, taking it out on the back porch. Staring into the brown liquid, he tried to decide how best to cut ties from Tori. He'd already planned to have their private plane take her wherever she needed to go, but he had to sever any and all notions of a relationship between them before it took root. It would be for the best.

He knew the moment she joined him on the porch. Her scent wrapped around him like a blanket, securing him, grounding him. She sat down next to him on the porch steps.

"Hey."

"Hi."

"You were up early."

"Yeah, I felt restless, I guess. The storm last night had me on edge."

A smile lifted the corners of her mouth, bowing her lips in a sweet grin. "I could have helped with that." Her hand came to rest on his arm, her touch sending heat straight to his groin.

Her hair was tousled, hanging around her shoulders in waves, giving her that just fucked look. The streaks looked like spun gold in the morning light. Her green eyes sparkled like dew in the grass. One of his old t-shirts covered her except for her tan legs, a feast for his eyes.

She bumped his shoulder with hers. "You okay?"

He took a sip of his coffee. A nod his only response.

They sat in silence for several moments. How exactly was he going to cut ties? He wanted this one last day though, to lose himself in Tori before he had to break her heart. "How about we pack a picnic and go riding today?"

"That sounds like fun."

"I have a few things to do around the house this morning, but we can go around noon."

"Perfect. I have to finish up my article and get it to you and the others so I can send it off to the publisher."

"Is it written?" he asked as they came to their feet.

"Mostly. I have to tweak a few things yet, otherwise yes it's done." She drained her coffee cup and turned to go back into the house. "You and the guys will see it before I turn it in. I promised, and I always keep my promises."

He watched her go back inside before leaving his cup on the step and heading down to the barn. The dingy interior reminded him of home. The one at his parents' place had been built many years after his. The property he owned dated back over a hundred years and the barn hadn't been updated much since then. Bare rafters filtered light through the slats above his head, leaving sunlight streaming across the floor. Dust particles floated around, dancing on the sunbeams.

Noah moved to the covered machinery in the corner, pulling the old tarp back to reveal a rusted plow. He didn't work the ground on his place, he didn't have time, but he wanted to make this old thing function more than anything he could remember doing. He'd always worked with his hands, helping his dad keep up the farming implements while he grew up. It had helped keep his mind clear of things that troubled his heart. Right now, he needed that.

Noon rolled around before he realized it when Tori found him in the barn elbows deep in grease and grime. She'd dressed in slim fitting jeans and a pink tank top that molded to her breasts like a lover's hand. He wanted nothing more than to smear the grease on his fingers along her breast so they could hide in the shower to wash it and his thoughts away with the soapy water. "Hey."

"Hi. You said noon, so here I am."

A honk sounded in the driveway. "And lunch has arrived," he said, wiping his hands on the rag he'd placed on the plow.

The grin lifting her lips tempted him to lean in and brush his mouth against hers. Unable to stop himself, he deepened the kiss as she wrapped her arms around his neck and moaned into his mouth.

The car honked again.

Noah pulled himself away from her addicting body, adjusting his hard cock behind the fly of his pants before moving toward the driver to pay him. "You are a witch."

The giggle escaping her lips made him smile a little wider. "How much?"

"Fifty-five twenty," the driver said as he put the cooler on the hood of the car. "The wine is in the pocket on the inside. The chicken is wrapped separately from the salad, the rolls, and the potatoes."

"Perfect. Thanks, man." Noah handed him a hundred dollar bill.

"Damn. You can call me anytime for a delivery if you always tip like that."

"Just remember. You don't know who I am, nor do you know where I live." He grabbed the red cooler, hanging it from his hand.

"You got it." The driver slid back inside his beat-up Toyota Corolla, disappearing down the driveway in a cloud of dust.

Noah brought his package back toward the barn. "I need to clean up a bit before we go." Tempted to ask her to join him in the shower, he resisted. Making love to her before he put his plan in motion tonight would be a real asshole move, although he wasn't sure he'd be able to stop himself.

"Sure. Is there anything I need to do?"

"Do you know how to ride?"

"Yeah, not very good, but I can stay on."

"There is tack in the room at the end. The saddles on the back wall should fit your size and the bridles next to them fit most of the horses. Pick something and bring it out to the center. I'll help you saddle a mare when I come back out." A quick kiss to her lips left him wanting more as he groaned and pulled away, leaving the cooler with their food on the table near the door. "Be back in a minute."

The warm spray of the shower helped ease the tension in his shoulders, but not the hardness of his cock, which stood straight up against his abdomen. The ache centered in his balls making him fully aware of the discomfort and wishing he'd brought Tori with him. He would just have to take care of it himself. The rapid rise of his desire had him coming all over his hand in seconds. It did little to stop him from wanting her.

Twenty minutes later, they rode out of the barn, him on a big bay gelding and her on a smaller black mare he knew she could handle. His intention was to take her back where he'd first kissed her. The water and the sand made for a great picnic area.

When they crested the hill, she sighed. "I love this place."

"I thought it would make you happy to see it again before you left tomorrow."

A shadow passed over her features, her eyes sad as they stared back into his. "I'm going to miss you guys."

Not sure how to respond without making things more difficult, he dismounted from his horse, tying him to a nearby tree before removing the picnic basket. "If you want to lay out the blanket, I'll get the food unpacked."

"Sure."

They worked in silence until everything had been laid out. Noah took the wine, opening it with the corkscrew he'd grabbed from the kitchen, before pouring a glass for Tori and one for himself. He raised his glass, clinking it together with hers. "To a successful article."

She smiled as she touched his glass with hers and then brought it to her lips to taste. "This is wonderful."

"I thought you might like it. It's from a small vineyard in Tennessee that I found a few years ago." He sipped his wine again for a second. "Let me fix you a plate. Are you hungry?"

Her eyes darkened with desire and need, something he knew well. She ran her tongue across her lips, taking the drop of wine that had lingered there. Her lips parted on a sigh, drawing him like a moth to a flame as he leaned closer. "Tori."

"Noah."

He ran his hand down her arm, lacing his fingers with hers. "I shouldn't touch you, shouldn't need you." Blood rushed in his ears. His heart pounded in his chest, thumping hard against his ribs. Breathing became a commodity, one he would have sworn was in short supply at that moment.

"Need me. Lord, please need me."

The moment their lips touched, he was gone, completely lost with no way out. Lost in her. Lost in the seconds as they ticked by. A soft moan escaped her lips as he ran his mouth along her cheek to her ear. With the lobe between his teeth, he nipped at the soft skin until her hands grabbed his biceps, digging her nails into his flesh. Not touching her wasn't an option anymore.

Her top left her skin bare to his mouth, his tongue, and his teeth. Little nips at her shoulder had her whimpering her desire as his name escaped her lips. Nothing in the world prepared him for the sound.

As he slipped the straps of her top down to expose her breasts to his gaze, he kept telling himself over and over how wrong he was, how he didn't need to hurt her more. The plea in her voice when she reached for his shirt silenced the voices until nothing could be heard except their excited breaths and the wind in the trees above them.

They tore at their clothes in a frantic race to get naked, his hands shaking as he reached for her to bring her beneath him. Their mouths crashed together in a wild gnashing of lips, tongues, and teeth. The slip of his tongue over hers drove his desire to the breaking point. He had to slow things down or he would come long before he was ready to.

He pressed his forehead to hers and opened his eyes. The emotion he read there ripped his heart in two. Falling for her wasn't an option in his world, he would only hurt her in the end, but this…this coming together would be imprinted on his mind and heart forever. "God, I need you."

With intimate touches and slow kisses, he ran his tongue and lips from the top of her shoulder, down her chest before stopping to lick, suck, and nip at her nipples, dragging a throaty cry from her mouth. Her breasts were so sensitive and responsive. Could he make her come from nipple stimulation only? Her nipples pulled into tight little buds, dark pink, and looking almost painful.

"Noah, please."

A pinch to her right one and his mouth on her left, made her arch her back, clutching at the back of his head to hold him there.

"OhGod, ohGod, ohGod." Her raspy cries of delight made his balls ache to be inside her.

Working his way down, he parted her silky thighs with his shoulders before nipping at the soft skin of her inner thighs. Her whimper had him smiling against her skin. The scent of her arousal drove him crazy with need.

Spearing his tongue, he slipped it over her clit as her hands fisted in his hair. Shoving both hands under her ass, he brought her closer to his mouth, loving first one side of her hard little nub and then the other until she was crying out in desperation to let her come.

"I need to come. Please."

The second he pushed two fingers into her hot center and flattened his tongue against her clit, she screamed his name as she flooded his mouth with her sweetness. He continued to lick and suck at her clit until she stopped quivering beneath him.

His jeans lay close, his wallet having slipped out of the back pocket, the condom he carried inside peeking out from the fold. Unable to wait to be inside her, he grabbed at the foil package, tore it with his teeth, and sheathed himself in a matter of seconds.

Her legs wrapped around his waist as he positioned himself at her opening and slowly pushed inside. "Hot. So fucking hot and wet. God, you slay me." She fit like a glove, so tight and warm, he wasn't going to last.

The soft whimpers coming from her mouth, the begging, and his name on her lips, he knew she was close again. Pressing his thumb down on her clit, escalating her breathing while he started to pound into her fast and hard.

"Yes. Fuck yes."

"Come with me, pretty girl. Let me feel you squeeze me."

Her pussy clamped down on him like a vise, pulling his orgasm from the base of his spine until he was grunting through his climax, her name a prayer on his lips.

After a few minutes, their breathing returned to normal while he rested his head on her shoulder. When he lifted his head, she grinned a wide dimpled smile and said, "Ready for chicken?"

* * * *

Music blared from the huge speakers in the corner as Tori settled in next to the guys in a corner booth. They'd made it to Rudy's in time to still get a table, but the place was packed with people like sardines. Sweat, perfume, and arousal hung like a blanket in the air, almost stifling, but exciting nonetheless.

A leggy brunette stopped at their table with her tray and a smile. "Drinks?"

Everyone ordered something, the guys a pitcher of beers, and for her an Alabama Slammer. She didn't drink often, but with the knowledge she was leaving tomorrow, her heart wasn't in a good place tonight. She'd finished her article, although she hadn't sent it to the guys yet, scared that she'd done something wrong and they would hate it. They'd become friends to her in the short time she'd been around them.

"So, Tori, what time are you leaving tomorrow?" Alex asked, tapping his fingers on the table.

"I don't know. Noah is having the pilot take me home in your plane."

Alex nodded before his gaze shifted to a blonde girl walking by, her skirt short enough to show her ass cheeks.

Dylan grinned and shook his head while Aiden rolled his eyes.

Dylan tapped her on the shoulder to get her attention as he leaned in close to her ear. "Is your article done?"

"Yes. You all will get a copy soon so you can give me your feedback."

"Awesome."

Noah sat next to her, but he seemed preoccupied, his gaze darting everywhere around the bar. He hadn't talked to her since they arrived, and he hadn't even held her hand or anything since they'd made love that afternoon. *Did I do something wrong?* His indifference made her frown as she sipped the drink the waitress had brought a moment before. *Should I say something to him?*

"Your boss wasn't mad you were here for the last two weeks, was he?" Aiden took a sip of his beer, his breath smelling like hops when he got close.

"No. He understood what I came to do." Her fingers traced the condensation on her glass. This was the first time since she'd been here, she felt completely out of place. The rest of the guys were as cordial as they usually were, but something felt off. Holding her breath for a second, she slid her hand onto Noah's thigh. His gaze collided with hers, fear, desperation, and sorrow reflected in the depths.

"I...uh...I'll be back." He shot to his feet, disappearing into the crowd.

"What the hell?" Alex said, his gaze stopping on her.

She shrugged as she went back to sipping her drink.

The music seemed to get louder, thudding so hard, her chest took the brunt of the beat. People milled about, mixing and mingling as they talked and laughed. Unsure of what was going on, Tori ordered another drink and sat back to listen.

After thirty minutes, she needed to use the restroom, so she slid out of the booth and headed toward the back. The bathrooms in these places weren't always the cleanest.

A long hall led toward the door at the end where a line, two women deep, stood waiting to get in. *Always the case. Never a line for the men's room.*

"Wow. It's crazy in here tonight." A brunette with a pixy cut stood at the front, her sparkly red skirt and white blouse bright enough to reflect the dim lighting.

Her friend tapped her on the arm. The girl could stop traffic with her boobs and the low cut dress she wore. The thing barely reached mid-thigh. "Yeah, but I bet you don't know why."

"Not really. This is busier than usual."

"The guys are here."

"Guys?"

"Yeah, Iron Rogue. They are in a corner booth. Someone said they might play."

"Aren't they on some kind of break?"

"True, but when they're in town, they tend to jam here sometimes. Tonight is our lucky night, I guess."

The brunette pushed open the door as her friend followed inside. "Maybe it is our turn. I would love to get Alex between my thighs."

"Not me. I have a thing for long, dark hair and a body built for me to lick. Noah has my engine jumping and right now, he's hanging near the bar so we need to hurry."

Tori stood with her mouth hung open for a second before she went inside. The two other women were further down the bathroom stalls, making it impossible for her to hear more of their conversation. It didn't matter. The leash on Noah had slipped off somewhere between the creek and the bar.

After washing her hands, she went back out into the crowded floor looking for Noah. He needed to tell her what the hell was going on before she ran too many scenarios through her mind. Either he wanted her or he didn't, and he needed to clarify.

The moment she rounded the bar, the sea of bodies parted leaving her a clear view. Noah stood near the end, his arm wrapped around the woman from the bathroom. Her short black dress hung off one shoulder, almost baring her breast for everyone to see. A row of shot glasses sat in front of Noah on the bar, a salt shaker and a bowl of limes next to them.

The girl grabbed the salt, pulled Noah's shirt away from his neck, sprinkling the salt on his skin before she grabbed the shot glass. With a toss of her head, she downed the liquid, licked the salt from his flesh, and pulled a lime from the bowl. Noah gave her his signature grin and dove in, taking the lime from between her lips as their mouths crashed together.

Tori couldn't breathe.

"My turn," she heard him say as he sprinkled salt on the swell of the girl's breast, picked up the glass before downing the shot and putting a lime between his teeth, daring her with his eyes to come and get it.

When he stopped kissing her, he looked over her shoulder, his gaze connecting with Tori's. A frown pulled his eyebrows down for a second before he broke contact and his lips lifted in a small smile.

With her heart shattered in her chest, she spun on her heels and headed for the door. *I don't care. I don't care. I don't care.* God, she wished it were true.

She grabbed a cab sitting outside the bar, telling him to take her to Noah's. She'd get her stuff and be gone long before he got home, if he came home. His spare key under the flowerpot would let her in, and she'd grab a cheap room in town. She didn't want him, his money, or his help. Fuck him. She was done. She'd get her own way home, and she'd never see the bastard again, so help her God.

Chapter Nine

"What in the fuck is your problem, Noah?" Alex asked as he pushed Noah's shoulder, shoving the woman away.

"Hey."

"Beat it."

The girl glared at Alex for a moment before she flipped her hair over her shoulder and stomped over to where her friend stood off to the side.

"I don't know what you're talking about, Alex."

"I fucking just saw Tori hightail it out of here like her ass was on fire. I came over here to see what was going on and find you playing lick suck with some bimbo."

"What's going on?" Dylan asked, sliding to a stop next to them.

"Noah's an asshole, that's what."

"Huh?" Aiden got close enough to hear what was being said.

"I don't need her, Alex, and it's best if she knows that up front."

"You can't be fucking serious?" Dylan's eyes narrowed with disappointment. "You hurt her? You really are an asshole."

"I'm not discussing this here in front of all these people. Let's go."

"Go where?"

"I'm going home. If you want a piece of me, do it there. Tori will be locked in her room, I'm guessing." Noah tore his keys from his front pocket, heading for the door. He felt like shit for hurting Tori, but it had to be done. She wasn't cut out for the life he had and serious relationships weren't his thing, never would be.

The moment he pulled up to the house, he knew something wasn't right. All the lights were off and it was too quiet. "Tori?" he called as he walked toward the room he'd given her. He opened the door and knew what was different. She was gone. "Tori?" He raced through the house, checking every room until he had to come to the final conclusion.

He left tracks through his hair as he slumped into the leather chair in the living room. The others in the band stood near the fireplace with their hands on their hips.

"How could you hurt her like this, man?" Dylan asked. "She's a nice girl."

"Yes, she is, and she doesn't need an asshole like me, okay. She needs a straight-laced guy who will love her, give her babies, and buy her a cute little house with a picket fence. She needs a guy who will be home every night, not some drunken rock star who wouldn't know love if it bit him on the ass."

Alex paced near the front windows, his lips drawn and his face a mask of rage. "I don't know much about love either, but what you did tonight was wrong. If you had an agreement and she knew there was nothing serious between you, then whatever. That's not what I saw in her eyes tonight, Noah. She cares about you, a lot. If you are too much of a fucking idiot to see it, you need your head examined." Alex slammed out the front door, his car spraying gravel as he tore off down the driveway.

Aiden sat in the chair across from him, his gaze fixed on Noah's face.

"What?"

"Nothing. I'm trying to decide if I should call a psych ward and have you committed or call the press and declare you to be in love."

"I'm not in love with Tori, Aiden. We had some good times while she was here, nothing more. She understood that. I made it clear from the beginning she didn't mean anything to me."

"Anything? Nothing at all?"

Noah couldn't look him in the eyes. He knew she meant more than any other woman he'd ever been with. "No. Nothing."

"You're a fucking liar, too. I can see it in your eyes, but if you aren't man enough to make her yours, then you can go on being the pussy of the group." Aiden slowly climbed to his feet, heading for the door. "If you want to talk, call me. Otherwise, there's a bottle of Jack in your cupboard. I put it there the other day when Tori was out doing her interviews with the others and you were prowling the streets until she was done. I have a feeling you'll need it before the end of the night." A look over his shoulder before he walked out told Noah nothing had gotten past his friend.

Dylan stood by the end of the couch where Noah had fucked Tori over the arm. His mind scrambled as those images came back, haunting him with how she'd let him take her without any regard to her feelings, because he needed the release.

"You know, I thought I knew you, Noah. I really did, but this person you've become has me baffled. You say you don't love her. The look on your face as you raced around the house looking for her a few minutes ago, tells me something different. Do you have any idea where she is?"

"No."

"Do you even know where she lives? I mean, the jet was supposed to take her home tomorrow, right?"

"Yeah, but I don't have a clue to where. She never mentioned it. In fact, I know very little about her where she knows a shit ton about me…about all of us."

"Well, you know who she works for. It's a start if you want to find her."

"I don't want to find her, Dylan. She needs to find someone who is right for her, and I need to go back to fucking every woman who crosses my path." He got to his feet to find the bottle of Jack Aiden said he'd left. After the third cupboard door proved to be the right one, he took his seat back in the chair and tipped the liquor to his mouth. The burn of the alcohol took his breath away.

"You could have waited until she went home to be an ass and break her heart."

"I could have, but I didn't. The break needed to be final and that's what I did."

"I don't know what else to say."

"Say nothing. Go on home. I'll see you guys at practice on Monday at the warehouse."

The door closed softly behind Dylan, leaving Noah alone in the silent house. The clock ticked by the seconds and minutes while he stared into the darkness down the hall where his room was. He couldn't go there. She would be everywhere, in his bed, in his shower, in his heart.

* * * *

Who the fuck turned on the sun?

A splitting headache roared behind his eyelids as bright light hit his face. He'd passed out across his bed, the pillow Tori had slept on pressed to his chest. The scent of her shampoo surrounded him as he let blissful, alcohol-induced sleep take him. He hadn't been sober since she'd left on Friday.

His mouth felt like something had crawled in there and died, leaving behind a smelly carcass.

The annoying ring of his cell phone buzzed as it raced across the nightstand where he'd left it three days ago. He didn't care to answer it, nor did he give a shit who was calling now.

What the hell day is it, anyway?

Mumbling under his breath, he finally decided to reach for the phone when he remembered he had a rehearsal Monday. When the screen finally came into focus after he blinked several times, he cussed under his breath as he noticed how many missed calls and texts there were.

The time was ten a.m. and the date showed Monday. *Fuck.* He was supposed to be at rehearsal at eight.

The phone buzzed again, showing Alex's smiling face. "What!"

"Noah? Where the hell are you, man? You're supposed to be at the warehouse."

He pressed his palm to his forehead. "I'm home lying across my bed in the clothes I've been wearing since Friday."

"You okay?"

"No. I've been drunk since she left, Alex. I even drove to town and got more whiskey. I haven't eaten, shaved, or showered in three days."

The slam of a door came through the phone and echoed through his head. "I'll be there in five."

Noah pushed up on his elbow and rolled over so he could stare at the ceiling for a moment. "It's okay. I'm fine. Give me half an hour and I'll be there."

"Are you sure?"

"Yeah, yeah." His eyelids were gritty and dry. *God, I need a shower.* "You guys work on something and I'll be right there."

"Okay. Be careful driving. Hangovers suck."

He clicked off the phone and rested it on his chest for a second. What had his life become in three days? This was not like him at all. The pitiful, guy who couldn't think past losing a woman. What the hell was up with that?

Rolling off the bed, he landed on his knees realizing his clothes stank, his boots were dirty, and his hair hung in a stringy, long mess down his face. As he pushed himself up, he staggered into the bathroom and turned on the shower before reaching for the buttons on the front of his shirt. A spot of something on the right side made him press his lips together when he realized it was dried puke. *Shit.*

The floor of the bathroom had droplets of vomit strung across until they blended with the bottom of the toilet. He'd apparently gotten sick at some point, but he couldn't remember exactly.

Vague memories filtered in, bringing back the loneliness and desperation he'd felt the moment he realized Tori had left without even a goodbye.

After I fucked up her head and her heart, it's no wonder.

Head swimming and naked as the day he was born, he stepped under the hot spray of the shower, letting his head fall back and the water cascade over his skull hoping it would relieve some of the pressure behind his eyes. After a few minutes, he grabbed some shampoo and poured some in his palm.

Fuck me. Tori's shampoo scent reached his nose.

The bottle hit the tile wall with a thud, splattering shampoo all over the inside of the shower.

God, this is pathetic. I have never been this screwed up over a woman. Why her? She's nothing special, right? Never mind she's gorgeous, funny, calls me on my shit, organizes my life, fits me like a glove, and makes me feel whole.

"I can't keep on like this. I have to get past this."

He finished his shower, sucked down a cup of coffee, and headed to the warehouse. They had work to do. Their break would be finished before he knew it, and they had nothing really to show for it. One new song, but it was a sappy ballad and not something their fans would like to start a new album. He needed to come up with a new hard-rocking set of lyrics, something that would bring them to their knees.

When he walked through the doors, he could hear the guys working on some of their older stuff, songs that were the mainstay of their performances. Each song meant something to him, brought back memories, or just made him feel good.

The first chords of Dare to Love hit Alex's guitar. Noah stopped in his tracks. It was the song that made the band, the song that until that moment had been something totally different to him. Now, the lyrics had a whole new meaning.

Staring out the window
The storm rages on
The image of you is not clear
Will I ever find you or are you just gone

Should I Dare to Love
Should I find someone else
Should I waste myself on the wrong one
Or should I wait for you

Time forever runs
With the shifting of the shadows
I can almost see you
Surrounded by the green of meadows

Should I Dare to Love
Should I find someone else
Should I waste myself on the wrong one
Or should I wait for you

You are here
Sent from above
On a wing and a prayer
Forever my love

Noah hung his head. Every line, every note, every word. From the beginning, he'd never known who he had written those lyrics for. His fans wanted to know. Tori wanted to know. Everyone had bets on what those lyrics meant. They didn't mean a damned thing…nothing. They were nothing more than a teenage boy's wish for the future, his future, what he wanted in the woman he would eventually fall in love with. He had always been searching, each face, each set of eyes for her and when he'd had her, he'd let her go.

Should I waste myself on the wrong one?

He had for years. He'd wasted so much time looking for her, he had almost missed her.

Now, how the hell did he fix this?

* * * *

The afghan across her legs did nothing to ward off the chill in her apartment. She'd been back in Los Angeles for three days. If felt like months. The silence surrounded her except for the ticking of the clock on the wall. Horns blared outside her window. People shouted. The smell of the city felt suffocating even in the park where she spent the last few days trying to find herself, her zest for life.

The phone call to her mother to get the plane ticket home was the worst mistake of her life. She hadn't heard the last of it, she knew. Without a choice in the matter, she'd called and begged for the money for the last minute flight. The lecture she'd endured for two hours solid about taking off without telling anyone where she was would have been the death of her except for her ability to tune out her mother.

The End.

She'd completed the article on Iron Rogue. The bones of it had been done in Iowa, but she'd finished polishing it a few moments ago.

Her email was open. Each one of the email addresses typed and ready to send so the guys could review it.

She couldn't hit send. She didn't want to see any response from Noah.

The tears had already come and gone. She had no more to cry or so she thought as one more raced down her cheek.

"Damn you!"

With the heel of her hands pressed against her eyes, she sobbed until she had nothing else to give. He didn't care. That appeared obvious as he took body shots off the other woman at the bar, his eyes locked on Tori's. He knew she'd seen, and he didn't give a shit. Jealousy had clawed at her gut, scratching her insides raw until she thought she'd lose her mind. Her chest ached with each thought of his lips on someone else. Nothing had prepared her for this.

The box of tissues at her elbow now gone, she wearily climbed to her feet to get another from the bathroom. She had to get past this so she could get the article turned it.

The fresh box tucked under her arm, she returned to the couch and picked up her cell phone as she pressed erase on the emails under the to be sent area.

"Rock Band News, can I help you?"

"Hi. Can I speak to Blaine, please?"

"Can I say who is calling?"

"Victoria Richmond."

"One moment please."

The phone clicked in her ear as music started to play. Her heart plummeted as Dare to Love sounded in her ear.

"Victoria, sweetheart. Are you all right? I've been worried since I haven't heard from you in several days."

"I'm fine. Back in Los Angeles and the article is done."

"Done as in finished?"

"Yeah."

"Did you get the background on the lyrics? That will seal the front page on this."

She closed her eyes, picturing Noah, his grin, the way his eyes darkened when they made love, the way he'd held her gently against his chest as they came down from their climax, and the look on his face as he licked that woman's breast. "Sort of."

"What do you mean, sort of?"

"Let me send you what I have. I told the guys I would let them read it before it was printed. You have to promise me you'll email it to them and let them see it before it hits the stands."

"Sure, doll. Anything."

Tori changed the destination email to Blaine's at the magazine and hit send. "It's on the way."

Silence on the line for a moment made her hold her breath. "Got it. I will send it to them right now."

"Thanks, Blaine."

"Welcome, babe. Are you coming in tomorrow?"

Her gaze went to the article on her laptop. Every last line seemed more personal than anything she'd ever written. It was the guys at their worst and their best. It was what she knew their fans wanted. The lines of Dare to Love came into focus on the page. Noah hadn't told her what they meant. Her own interpretation lined the article. Once he read what she'd written, he would never speak to her again. *Perfect. I don't need him.* Why didn't she believe that? "Yeah. I'll be at my desk in the morning. I just need...I need today to unpack and get some things straight before I get back to work."

"I'll see you in the morning then."

"Yeah."

The phone clicked off before she set it down on the table, her palms sweaty. With a little luck, the article would be a hit and her career set. Travel to and from concerts could become her life, interviewing bands, making them popular with her information, and giving them the notoriety they deserved. She would find some nice safe guy, settle into life touring the country with all the perks of being the best damned reporter in rock band history.

Why did it sound so lame?

Because it wouldn't be Noah in the bed next to her every night.

She leaned against the back of the sofa, covering her eyes with her arm. It didn't matter what she wanted or needed when it came to that stubborn asshole with the gorgeous eyes and killer mouth. He didn't want her. He'd made that perfectly clear.

Just picturing the look in his eyes before he'd lean in and bring their mouths together made her whole body hum with tension. He knew how to kiss better than any man she'd ever known. The subtle thrust of his tongue dancing with hers, the way their mouths crashed together sometimes like they couldn't get enough of one another, the little kisses he'd press to the edges of her mouth early in the morning right before he'd slowly push inside her, and God help her, the way he'd stare into her eyes as he loved her with everything he had.

The man knew exactly what to do to bring her orgasm in moments, but he was the master of holding her climax at bay until *he* was ready to let her come. They'd spent so much time talking, laughing, and getting closer while she'd been in his home, she had been sure there was something there. A look when he thought she didn't notice, a brush of his mouth on the back of her neck when she was doing dishes, his fingers sliding gently over the insides of her thighs right before he brought his lips to her center. The moment he'd push his cock into her and pull her legs up high on his hip so he could get as deep as possible.

How was she ever going to get over him?

Wine.

A whole bottle. Maybe more than one if she had to.

An hour later she was three sheets to the wind. Her words slurred and her vision unfocused as she wiggled the now empty bottle in front of her eyes. *Well hell.*

Her cell phone rang a few minutes later, the ringtone telling her it was Bella. She wasn't sure she really wanted to talk to her friend right now, but she did need to let her know she was back in Los Angeles. "Bell, Bell. What's up girl?"

"Tori?"

"Yep. Tori. That's me."

"Are you okay? You sound, I don't know…"

"Drunk? Because yes I might be. I had a bottle of wine."

"You mean a glass, right?"

"Nope. The entire bottle."

"I'll be there in five minutes. You are home, aren't you?"

"Yes," she whispered, the desperation creeping into her voice. Tears threatened to close her throat. "I hate that bastard, Bella."

"Stay put. I'll be right there."

Tori had barely hung up the phone when her friend burst through the door, enveloping her in the arms of a friend who would understand.

Bella patted her back as she poured tears down the front of her shirt. "I hate him."

"Who, honey? Who do I have to kill for you?"

Tori shook her head. She didn't want to even utter his name, the pain of it would kill her. "He tore my heart out and stomped on it. It doesn't matter if he looked at me like he might have feelings for me when we made love. I swear they were there, Bell. He couldn't have made love to me like that and not felt something, right?" Her fists were clenched in her friend's t-shirt as she desperately searched Bella's eyes for confirmation. "Right?"

"Ah, sweetie. Noah got to you, didn't he?" Bella cupped her face, wiping the tears streaming down Tori's cheeks.

"I hate that rat bastard!"

"I know. He'll get his. Someday he'll fall in love with someone and she'll stomp on his heart like he did yours."

Great hiccupping sobs broke from her lips. "I don't want him to love someone else. I want him to love me."

Bell held her against her chest for what seemed like a long time. "Let me get the other bottle of wine I saw sitting on your kitchen counter. This calls for a wicked hangover in the morning. Then you'll be ready to put that asshole behind you and find the man you were meant to be with. The one who will love you for everything you are and treat you like a princess." Bella grabbed the wine, pouring them both a healthy glass. "To Noah. May his heart rest in peace."

The next morning the shrill of her cell phone pulled her from a wine induced sleep. "All right. All right. I'm coming." Without looking at the caller ID, she grabbed the phone and groggily answered.

"What in the fuck have you done?"

She pulled the phone from her ear before glancing at the screen and then putting it back up to her ear. "Noah?"

Chapter Ten

"God damn it, Tori! You said you'd let us read the article before you published it."

The whistle of sucking air through her teeth echoed in her bedroom. What was he talking about? She'd done what she said. "I did. I had Blaine send it to you."

"Then why is it front page on the magazine on the newsstands this morning?"

She could tell he was pacing from the sounds of his footfalls. "I don't understand."

"My producer called first thing this morning. The entire article is already all over the web. The phones are going nuts in his office because of the shit you printed."

"I swear, Noah. I didn't print anything. I wrote it, yes, but I called Blaine and told him to send it to you guys for review."

"Why didn't you send it?"

The sting of the bite she placed on her lower lip reminded her to talk. "I didn't want to talk to you after what went down in Sommerton since you obviously didn't give a shit about hurting me."

"I told you what my life was like, Tori. I never hid that from you."

Her phone beeped with a text message from Bella. *I don't know what you did with that article, but be prepared when you go outside. The bellman has kept them from coming up, but the paparazzi are swarming.*

"What the hell?" she whispered as she peered out her window. There must have been twenty reporters down there at the door.

"You need to retract that article, Tori. I will not have the band smeared all over the place like this."

"I didn't write anything that wasn't true, Noah."

"No? Then why is the caption on the front *The real inside track to the lyrics for Dare to Love*? I never told you what those lyrics meant. Did you just make up some shit to print?"

"I—"

"You know what? Never mind. You'll hear from our attorney." The click in her ear was deafening and final.

Her next call went to Blaine.

"Good morning, Miss Celebrity. You are the hot commodity this morning."

Anger seethed through her, making her stomach clench so badly she thought she'd be sick. "What in the hell have you done, Blaine? You printed that article without the band having read it and approved it, didn't you?"

"Babe, this is business. The article was fantastic. It was everything the fans were looking for and you, you are the woman of the hour. The magazines are flying off the shelves. The hits on the website are in the millions. I've heard from the band's PR person and she says the event planners are asking for more dates. Iron Rogue will be more popular than ever, thanks to you."

"No. Now they will hate me," she whispered as she hung up the phone. She was due at the office already and she didn't have a choice. A quick shower would have to do. Facing that mob downstairs and the fallout at the magazine would take up her entire day and it was something she didn't want to face. She'd hurt Noah.

The paparazzi were crazy when she opened the front door of her apartment building, yelling questions, flashing cameras, and sticking microphones in front of her face. Trepidation rolled down her back. She didn't want to deal with this, any of this, but she'd brought it on herself by trusting Blaine.

"Ms. Richmond. Is it true Noah King told you the meaning of the lyrics of Dare to Love?"

"No comment." She side-stepped the woman asking the question, only to be blocked by a man wearing a rock t-shirt and jeans with rips in them. His blonde hair fell into his eyes, giving him a boyish appearance until he opened his mouth.

"Is it true you spent two weeks living under the same roof with him? Maybe there is more to your article than meets the eye."

Anger rushed through her at their audacity. They were reporters, yes, but digging into her time spent with Noah had nothing to do with her article or the information she'd gathered. God, was this what the guys put up with all the time? The constant ripping apart of their personal lives and what they ate for breakfast? "How dare you. What goes on in my personal life is none of your business. Where I spent the last two weeks is not your concern, and I would hope any further questions concerning that time frame will not be asked. If you'll excuse me, I have to be at work." Her quick steps took her to the parking garage where she'd left her car as she disappeared through the locked door and breathed a sigh of relief. *This better blow over quickly or I'm going to kill Blaine. That weasel will pay for this.*

Several moments later, the whoosh of the main doors opening ruffled her bangs as she stepped through them, the heels of her boots clicking on the floor.

"Good morning, Tori. It's nice to see you back," the receptionist said when she came in. The woman had been with the magazine for over ten years and did her job well, keeping out the people who shouldn't be in the building especially when a band came in for a television interview.

"Good morning, Minnie. You look fabulous as always."

Minnie primped her hair a little and grinned. "Awesome article. You kicked-ass on that one. It's the talk of the building."

Tori wanted to tell her something, anything that would kill the buzz, but she couldn't. The information in the article was the truth, or most of it was anyway, unless Blaine had altered it before it went to print. *Holy shit. I'd better read it myself to make sure he didn't.*

A print copy of the magazine sat on the reception desk on the corner, so she grabbed one and rolled it up as she walked to the elevator to get to her office. She needed to read it quickly before she talked to Blaine.

Inside her office, she shut the door and took the chair behind her desk as she booted up her computer. The hits on her article were important to her, like they'd always been, but today she might need a drink before she looked even though it was only ten in the morning.

The front of the magazine caught her eye, making her heart beat wildly in her chest. It was a picture of the whole band from the photo shoot they'd done at the warehouse when she'd been in Sommerton. She recognized the inside stage as if she stood right there in front of them. They were lost in the music, each looking straight at the camera with a different emotion shimmering in their eyes. Alex had his typical smirk resting on his lips, the one that brought women to him in droves. Aiden looked lost in the rhythm of his guitar, his gaze fixed on a spot over the photographer's shoulder. Dylan had sweat pouring down the side of his face, but she could see the love for the music in the upswing of his sticks and the tilt of his head.

Noah. God, Noah. His eyes held her transfixed. Emotions swam in his gaze as he held the microphone in his palm, his head tipped slightly to the right, his hair resting on the right side of his chest, and his lips lifted in a tiny grin. She'd seen that look way too many times to realize at that very moment, he'd been looking at her.

A deep breath escaped her lips the moment she opened the magazine and began to read. Her blood began to boil at the embellishments Blaine had taken it upon himself to include in *her* article.

"Noah King, the lead singer for the band Iron Rogue, wrote the lyrics for Dare to Love—

She continued to read, getting more pissed off with each change she read. Blaine had even gone to the extent of making up something about the lyrics. That had not been included in the article she'd sent him because it hadn't existed.

By the time she'd finished, her blood pressure was through the ceiling, her heart was hammering in her chest, and her palms were sweaty. The article had to be retracted, and it would be if she had anything to say about it.

With a plan in her head, she opened the door and walked down the hall to Blaine's office. Her knock received a commanding come in.

"Tori, I'm glad you're here." He motioned to the chair across from his desk, indicating she should sit down. "Mr. Walker, I have you on speaker phone, and Tori is here in my office."

"Victoria, I'm thrilled with the article. I've been talking to Blaine for the last few minutes about where your career is going and where it should go from here. I'm not sure if you're aware, but there is a head reporter position available within the magazine, and I think you would be a perfect fit. It comes with a substantial pay raise, of course, a generous expenditure account for travel, and of course the title, which would open many doors."

Tori was speechless. She had no idea there was a head reporter position available, much less that she was being considered for it. She got to her feet, leaned over Blaine's desk, and clicked off the phone effectively hanging up on the owner of the magazine. "*You* are the biggest ass hole I've ever had the misfortune of working with. You twisted my words, changing at least half the meaning of that article to suit what you thought would sell magazines. The guys from the band never had a chance to okay that article like I promised. I do not fucking believe you!"

A greasy smile lifted the corners of his lips. "I don't understand, Tori. This is what you wanted, right? You wanted a kick-ass career as a rock band reporter. You've done it. It is in the bag, babe, but you need to get over these soft feelings for your interviewees. What we have here is strictly for the good of the magazine."

"What you've done is completely unethical, Blaine. These guys are real people with families and lives outside of being on the stage. Do you have any idea of what you've done?"

Blaine's face was now flush red, anger, making the veins in his neck stand up. "I did what I had to do for the magazine. You should take lessons from what this means."

Tori leaned forward on the desk, placing her palms flat on the surface as she got nose to nose with Blaine. "You *will* retract that article."

"I absolutely will *not*. The sales of the magazine have blown every record we have. I'm sure you've seen the hits on the article. Your career is made. I don't understand what your problem is."

Her voice dropped to a mere whisper. "I'm not giving you a choice, Blaine. You are an egotistical bastard who is only out for his own benefit. Don't give me this shit that everything you did was for the magazine or for me. None of it was for anyone but you as the editor in chief. You will sell thousands of magazine by doing this, in turn securing your own bonus this year."

His skin blanched a solid sheet of white.

"Did you think I didn't know? Did you think this would go unnoticed?" She straightened to upright. "This is going to bite you on the ass in the long run. I'll make sure of it." Her teeth were clenched so hard, she thought she'd crack a tooth.

"You can do nothing."

"Fine. I quit." She spun on her heel, pulled open the office door, letting slam against the wall. "By the way, you'll be hearing from Iron Rogue's lawyer. They plan on suing."

"Tori!"

She ignored the shouting from his office doorway.

"You're going to regret this."

Her middle finger shot to the ceiling with a one-finger salute in his direction. *Fucker.*

Ten minutes later, she walked out with one box under her arm, her entire life as a reporter enclosed under the cardboard flaps.

"What's going on?" Minnie asked, sprinting as fast as she could around her desk on her three-inch heels. "Where are you going?"

"I quit. I'm done."

"What? Seriously?"

"Yep and you can let everyone in the building know that I didn't write that article in its present form. Blaine took it upon himself to stuff it full of shit and print it. I interviewed the band, yes, but what's in that magazine is not my doing."

"Holy crap, Tori. I can't believe he did that."

"I can. He doesn't give a shit about anyone except himself. So, now I'm out of a job."

Minnie hugged her and stepped back. "If you need a reference, girl, let me know. You are the best reporter I know."

A sob escaped her lips for a second before she shored up her pride and smiled. "Thanks. I might take you up on that."

The stifling heat of Los Angeles hit her in the face the second she walked out of the doors and headed to the parking garage. It would be the last time she walked those halls, the last time she would park her car in spot number twenty-nine, and the last time she would wear her Rock Band News t-shirt to a concert.

I hope I've done the right thing.

As soon as she made it through her apartment door, she calmly set the box on the table near the wall, kicked off her shoes, and headed for the kitchen. *Surely it isn't too early for ice cream.* She grabbed the half-gallon carton of chocolate chip and a huge spoon, a teaspoon wouldn't do in this case. The biggest one she could find was a serving spoon used for soup. *Perfect.* She sat down on the couch, tucked her feet under her butt, and dug in. Later, she'd go for the wine and figure out what she was going to do to pay her bills. Without a job, that would prove difficult.

With the curve of the spoon face down, she ran her tongue over it to retrieve every bit of ice cream. She planned on eating the whole half-gallon to assuage her messed up life. Her cell phone pinged with a text from Bella. Not sure whether to let her friend know she was home, she let it lay near her knee, the screen mocking her to answer it.

By the time she was halfway through the carton, Bella had texted three more times.

The phone lit up with Bella's face. A heavy sigh escaped Tori's lips as she picked up the phone and hit talk. "Yeah?"

"What are you doing?"

"Eating a half-gallon of ice cream all by myself."

"What happened at work? I saw you come home within an hour of leaving."

"I quit."

"You quit? Why?" Bella asked, her voice a high-pitched, unbelievable tone.

What? Does she think I'm kidding?

A tear slid down her cheek at the loss of her life, her job, and even though she didn't want to admit it—Noah. "Because Blaine fucked me over. He put shit in the article that wasn't what I'd originally written. Noah called and threatened to sue me and the magazine, which I'm sure he will do. And God damn it, Bella. I love him."

"Oh, honey. I'm at work or I'd be right there. I'll come over as soon as I get off and we can commiserate together."

She sniffed, holding back the choking sob trapped in her throat. "I'll be okay. You don't have to come," she whispered, taking another spoonful of ice cream.

"Are you sure?"

Tori wiped her face with her sleeve, tempted to blow her nose on her blouse as she located the box of tissues she'd had yesterday. "Yeah. I have to figure this shit out myself. I'm not sure what I'm going to do for a job, but I'll think of something. I can always wait tables like I did in college." Her phone beeped in her ear. "Hang on, I have another call."

She glanced at the screen seeing an unknown Los Angeles number.

"Hello?"

"Is this Victoria Richmond?"

"Yes?"

"This is Abraham Noble. I am the owner of Lyric. I would like to talk to you about your article printed today."

Tori looked at the phone again before putting it back to her ear. "You're joking, right?"

"No. I can send you to my secretary if you don't believe me."

Disbelief made her heart beat faster, thundering loud enough in her ear, she wasn't sure she could hear a word. One, how the hell did the guy get her phone number, and two, why was he calling her? "Uh, okay. Give me a moment, please." She clicked over to Bella and told her she would call her back. "All right, Mr. Noble. What can I do for you?"

"Did you write the article in Rock Band News on Iron Rogue?"

"Yes and no, sir."

"Can you elaborate?" he asked, his voice deep and penetrating as he pushed for more information.

"I would rather not over the phone."

"Noted, Ms. Richmond. Would you be able to come into our offices tomorrow morning at nine? I would like to talk to you in person then."

Her heart plummeted. "Are you an attorney?"

A rumble of laughter echoed on the other end of the line. "No, Victoria. I am not. As I said, I am the owner of Lyric. I am interested in you as a reporter, and I would like to discuss putting you on my staff."

Chapter Eleven

The moment she stepped inside the all-glass building, she felt like throwing up.

As she rode the elevator to the top floor, she drew air in through her nose and out through her mouth, trying to calm her heart. *How in the hell did this happen? I'd never even heard of Abraham Noble before yesterday.*

The doors slid open, revealing a single desk with a woman sitting behind it. Her glasses were perched low on her nose, her hair was pulled back in a severe bun at the base of her neck, and her lips were pursed as if she'd sucked on a lemon.

"Can I help you?"

"I have an appointment with Mr. Noble at nine?"

"Your name?"

"Victoria Richmond."

"Have a seat. I'll let Mr. Noble know you are here."

With her butt perched on the edge of the ornate seat, she tapped her fingers on her bag where she'd put it on her lap. Her gaze wandered around the office, taking in the silver lining everything. The entire place was decorated in black and white, the chairs, the desk, the light fixtures, and the mirrors. *God, I am out of my element.* Not sure what to make of the phone call yesterday, she'd done some research on Lyric and found a picture of the owner who was indeed Abraham Noble. His father had started the magazine fifty years before and *everyone* in rock and roll knew Lyric.

Tori climbed to her feet and approached the desk. "I…uh—"

The door behind the woman opened and one of the most handsome men she'd ever seen, stepped out. "Ms. Richmond?"

He held out his hand for her to shake. "Please, come in. I've been looking forward to meeting you." His hair was dark with some silver at the temples, giving him a distinguished look. His blue eyes sparkled with laughter as his gaze skimmed over her from head to toe. Wide shoulders looked amazing in his tailored suit, along with his dark slacks, and black shoes.

Tori dumbly followed him through the doors, until he led her to a seat across from his desk. Surprisingly, he took the chair next to her rather than the one on the other side of the massive oak monstrosity.

"Call me Tori, please," she said after she'd cleared the fuzziness from her throat. "It is nice to meet you, Mr. Noble."

"Please, call me Abe." He laughed and patted her hand. "You have a very dubious look on your face."

She couldn't help but feel out of place. The man commanded the room with his presence. His large frame dominated the space with his height at over six foot.

"I'm sorry, Abe, but you have me at a disadvantage, I'm afraid."

Abe leaned over and grabbed something off his desk, flipping it over to reveal the cover of Rock Band News. "I read your article on Iron Rogue, and I had some questions for you."

"Oh?"

"Yes. First of all, where did you get your information?"

"From the guys."

His head tilted to the side as his eyes narrowed. "You personally interviewed the band?"

"Yes."

"After a show, I imagine."

"No, sir. Personally, very personally."

His left eyebrow went up as his lips tipped into a grin. "You indicated that not everything in that article was written by you."

"No. It was not. The editor in chief at Rock Band News decided to take my article and stretch the truth without my or the guys' knowledge. I had promised the band they would get to see the article before it was published. I had sent it to my boss to forward to them and instead, he tweaked the contents and published it." Tori wiped her sweaty palms on her skirt. "I'm sorry, Mr. Noble, but what does this have to do with me?"

"My understanding is you no longer work at Rock Band News, correct?"

Startled, she nodded slowly wondering where this was headed and who had told him she didn't work there anymore. This was all getting a bit weird.

Abe steepled his hands, his fingers under his chin. "Let me elaborate a little, Tori. I have an insider at Rock Band News. I've been watching you for some time actually, watching your career that is. You've a fantastic way with the bands, every one you've ever interviewed. Your articles are articulate and on point with what the fans want to know. You are a fantastic writer, giving just enough information, but always holding a little back for the next one."

Her brain was stuck on insider. "Insider?"

He laughed. "Minnie is my sister."

Holy shit! "Minnie the receptionist?"

"Yes. She called me the moment you walked out of the office yesterday with your box under your arm and told me if I didn't hire you, I was a fool. My sister *never* calls me a fool without good cause."

"Wait. I'm confused. You want to hire me?"

"I do. I want you on my staff, and you'll be exclusive to the new bands, interviewing them, getting into their heads, feeling out the songs, and giving us the best damned articles on rock and roll in the country."

"Oh my," she said, placing her hand on her chest. "I'm flabbergasted, to say the least. I mean, I quit Rock Band News yesterday and here today you are offering me a job?" Her mind spun from one thing to another, the travel, the pay, the benefits, and back to the pay again.

"The salary would be comprehensive with the work you will be doing. The travel is covered, of course, and we have a great benefits package." He climbed to his feet and went around the desk. Pushing a button on the phone, he said, "Can you have Barbara from human resources come in here please, and have her bring a standard contract."

A few moments later, a gorgeous woman with flaming red hair, came through the door, a packet of papers in her hand. "You asked for a contract, Abe?"

"Yes, Barbara. Thank you." He took the envelope and introduced her to Tori. "This is Victoria Richmond. I hope she'll take the job of New Band Reporter."

"Nice to meet you, Victoria. I hope you'll be happy here. If you have questions, my card is in the envelope. You can call me anytime."

"Thank you," Tori replied, taking Barbara's hand in a firm shake. "I appreciate that tremendously since I'm kind of at a loss right now."

Barbara laughed as she glanced at Abe. "He does tend to bowl people over sometimes."

When Barbara had left the room, Abe handed Tori the packet of paperwork. "I had this drawn up before you got here. It is negotiable to some degree, so feel free to look it over and let me know if you want to talk about anything." He held out his hand for her to shake. "I do hope you'll seriously consider our offer. I am looking forward to having you on our team."

At this very moment, she stood outside her car staring at the envelope in her hand until she screamed at the top of her lungs and began to do a happy dance right there in the parking garage of the magazine. She clutched the thick packet to her chest, scrunching her eyes closed as she felt a stupid grin spread across her face. Her heart raced along at ninety miles an hour, making her lightheaded. *I have a job at the biggest rock magazine in the country! Oh, my God. I might have just peed a little.* A giggle escaped her lips as she pushed the unlock button on her key fob and slipped inside her car. Bella won't believe this.

Her cell phone in hand, she snapped a selfie with the envelope titling it *New Job!* and sent it off to her friend.

The text that came back had *celebrating tonight?*

You bet, she typed back and hit send. Everything might work out after all.

Once she got home, she opened the envelope with some apprehension. What if the benefits package wasn't good enough? What if the salary was too low? What if? What if? What if? *This is ridiculous. Just open the damned thing.*

The moment she had the papers spread out on her dining room table, her eyes were drawn to the salary. *Holy shit!* It was even more than she was making at Rock Band News and the benefits were better too. *This is too good to be true.* She pinched her arm. "Ouch. I guess I'm not dreaming."

A hard knock on the door drew her gaze to the portal right before Bella bounced through the doorway. "So? They offered you a job?"

"Yes, and you won't believe this. The whole package is fantastic, Bella. Mr. Noble even said things were negotiable, but I can't see negotiating anything." She pushed the papers toward her friend. "Please, read this and tell me it is a good thing to take because I'm sitting here not believing this is for real."

Bella read over the contract word for word and sat back. "You haven't read this, have you?"

Tori's heart sank. "Not entirely, why? What's wrong with it?"

"You were swayed by the numbers and the benefits. I can tell by the look in your eyes."

Her stomach began to ache and her eyelids started to burn with tears. It wasn't real. It wasn't as good as she thought it was.

Something was wrong. She could tell by the look in Bella's eyes. "Just tell me," she whispered. "I can take it."

Bella took her hand. "Tori, it's a fantastic contract. The only thing you might have a problem with is that they want you to sign that you'll guarantee them two years of employment, but I don't see that as a problem for you. The salary is lucrative and everything else looks great too."

A high-pitched squeal ripped the air as Tori jumped to her feet and hugged her friend. "I knew I loved having you as a best friend and it helps that you're a paralegal."

"I would still have an entertainment attorney look at it for your benefit, just to be sure."

"I will, of course. I think I have the name of a couple of them from working at Rock Band News. It never hurts to know people." Tori did a little dance in her living room before hugging herself and giggling. "This is so awesome!"

"You never told me how Lyric got your name."

She grabbed Bella's hands. "Oh my God. You won't believe this, but Minnie the receptionist at the front desk, she is Mr. Noble's sister. She called him the minute I walked out those doors and told him if he didn't hire me, he was a fool."

"Wow."

"I know, right?" She took a deep breath and sank down on the couch. Her stomach knotted as she thought about what this new job entailed. She would be traveling a lot. She'd keep her apartment, but how often would she even be there? Thank God she didn't have any pets and the few plants she harbored, she could give to Bella. A look around her apartment brought tears.

"What's wrong?"

"I won't be here a lot. You know, this right?"

Bella pulled her into a hug. "I know, but we'll call and Skype. You'll be having so much fun running around the world, you won't even miss me."

"You aren't serious, are you? Of course, I'll miss you."

"Then you'll find some hunky guy to hook up with. You'll be so busy with your new life, I'll be a distant memory."

"Hunky guy?"

"Yeah. You know, famous rock star and all."

A tear slipped down her cheek before Bella could wipe it away. "I miss him, Bell."

"I know, sweetie, but it'll get better. I promise."

"What if it doesn't? What if I can't move on?"

"You will. Be strong. He's an asshole from the word go and doesn't deserve your love. Remember that, because you know what?" She pushed Tori's hair from her face and tucked it behind her ear. "You will run into him again someday, and you'll be able to shove it in his face that he had you once and lost you."

The thought of running into Noah again made her chest hurt. Being in his arms was her oasis, her port in the storm, and he was her everything for those two weeks. She couldn't blame him entirely. He had warned her, but that didn't make it hurt any less. Even if he didn't know it, she'd given him her heart.

* * * *

"Damn it!"

Alex pulled the last chord on his guitar and unstrapped it from around his back. "What the hell, Noah. The words are right there. You wrote them, for crying out loud, and you can't even get them straight once? Do we need to take a break?"

They were working on a new album. Some of the songs were picked. The guys knew their parts, but do you think he could get the damned words straight, no. *Mother fucker!*

This whole thing with Tori and the article had him in such a fucking mess, he couldn't think, much less get any kind of work done, writing or singing. He had a conference call with their attorney this afternoon, and he just wanted to get it over with. Once everything was filed, he could stop thinking about it and her.

"Yeah. Let's break for five, and we'll take it up again."

A bottle of Jack sat on the floor near his feet. It had become his lifeline, his escape, and his way to forget. Tipping the bottle to his lips, he took a long swig, feeling the burn of the alcohol as it went down his throat.

"You need to lay off that shit, brother," Dylan said as he walked past.

"Fuck you."

Dylan held up his hands and kept moving until he was outside the main doors, leaving Noah alone in the huge building. The echo of their footsteps stopped, leaving him in deafening silence. God, he hated silence these days. He was surrounded by it at home and now here.

She'd been gone a month, a whole month of this shit. He couldn't eat, he couldn't sleep, and he couldn't write lyrics if his life depended on it.

The article had been a boon for their careers, making them front page news on several magazines since it had hit the newsstands. Their record sales had spiked hard and ticket sales for their upcoming shows were sold out, many asking for more dates. The point was, what they'd written wasn't true or at least some of it wasn't. He wanted the record straight on those damned lyrics.

"You ready to go again?" Aiden asked as they came back inside.

"Yeah. Let's do this."

Aiden put his hand on Noah's shoulder. "Listen, man, if you need to quit for today, it's cool. We can try tomorrow to get some of these songs done."

"Thanks, man, but I'm good. I just have to cut in about an hour. I have an important call to take."

"No worries." Aiden slapped him on the back. "You got this and just for the record, I liked her too."

Aiden grabbed his bass, strapping it around his back as he got into position.

Noah took his spot behind the microphone, closed his eyes, and let the music take him away from everything going on. The song was a love ballad, the one he'd written when Tori was with him, and now he brought the lyrics up in his mind, pushing all thoughts but her from his head.

Each word, every phrase took a piece of his heart with it until the last chord drifted off. He'd fucked up and lost her because he was too stupid to realize she meant everything to him. The heat of her gaze, the touch of her skin beneath his lips, the feel of her wrapped around him as they made love—God he was an idiot.

The sound engineer busted through the booth door. "That was fucking awesome!"

Noah put the microphone back on the stand. "I've got to go, guys. I have something I have to take care of right now. I'll catch you tomorrow."

Keys in hand, he made his way out to his truck, started the engine, and roared off down the back road until he reached his house. This madness had to stop and it would, right now.

"Miller, Smith, and Mitchell. Can I help you?"

"Yes. This is Noah King. I need to talk to Hilbert Miller, please. It's important."

"One moment, please."

The line went to elevator music for a moment before a deep voice picked up the phone. "Noah, what can I do for you?"

"Hilbert. I need you to drop the suit against Victoria Richmond and Rock Band News."

"No can do, Noah. Papers are already filed." Tap, tap, tap. "I just checked the serving company, both parties were served this afternoon."

"Shit." He raked his fingers through his hair as he dropped down on the armchair in the living room of his house. "What can we do?"

"Do?"

"I don't want this suit to go through, Hilbert."

The other end of the line was silent for a moment. "I'm not sure what's going on with you and this thing, Noah, but if nothing else, we can go to mediation and talk to the magazine and Victoria to see what can be done. What exactly do you want to happen with this?"

"The only thing I really wanted was them to retract the article and admit they lied."

"Did they?"

He growled. "Yes. I never told anyone what was behind the lyrics for our song. They lied about that although I'm not sure if it was Tori or someone else at the magazine." He tipped his head back onto the rear of the chair. "I was pissed, Hilbert. She walked out without even a goodbye and then that shit came out."

"Let's call for mediation then and see what happens."

"I want to be there."

"Are you sure?"

"Yes."

"Done. I'll call their attorney and we'll set it up for two days from today. When do you guys go back on the road?"

"Our first show is in a month."

"How is your dad?"

Anger tightened his gut. He didn't want to think of losing his father, but it seemed to be coming faster than he was prepared for. "Not good. Things are progressing pretty fast. He can hardly get around these days. I'm doing everything I can to help."

"I imagine. Hang in there."

"Thanks." He sighed. "Let me know the specific date, time, and location for the mediation."

"Will do."

He clicked the phone off and laid it beside him on the arm of the chair. Tori. Damn if her name didn't still give him a rush, one straight to his heart. He'd never been wrapped up in a single woman before, but he'd come to realize things with her weren't normal. She'd been everything to him from the moment he'd held her hair back as she puked on the plane. Maybe he should call her. Thank goodness the magazine had given him her number when he'd asked, no matter he'd had to threaten someone's life to get it.

The gallery on his phone opened with a swipe of his finger and the picture he'd taken near the creek filled the screen. He could almost smell her scent in the room surrounding him, feel the texture of her hair when he'd run his fingers through it, and her lips... he could almost taste them.

His cell phone popped up a picture of his dad and his heart stopped. "What's up?"

It was his mom.

"You'd better come, Noah. Your dad is bad."

"I'll be there in five minutes."

He shot to his feet, grabbing his keys and his wallet on the way out the door. *God, please. I'm not ready for this.*

The truck hadn't even shut off when he launched himself from the cab and raced up the steps. "Mom?"

"In the bedroom, sweetie."

He pushed open the door and rushed to the side of the bed as his dad weakly opened his eyes. "Noah, son." His dad held out his hand. "Sit with me."

"Did you call the others?" he asked, glancing at his mother before his gaze went back to his dad. The pale frail man in the bed wasn't his father. The man before him was nothing like the robust, barrel-chested rancher his father had been.

"Yes, but they can't be here until tomorrow."

Noah pulled up a chair, sliding his butt onto the seat as he leaned forward. "Pop?"

His dad coughed, a rough, hard, rattling sound Noah hadn't heard before. The tissue pressed to his lips had speckles of blood on it. *When did this happen?*

"My time is coming to an end, Noah, but I want you to do something before I take my last breath."

"Anything, Pop." His dad meant the world to him and whatever he wanted him to do, he'd take care of it in a heartbeat.

His dad's eyes sparkled in the overhead light as he looked right at Noah and said, "Make up with that pretty little lady you had here and find the love I know is in your heart."

Noah pushed a breath out roughly for a moment. His thoughts went to Tori and then he got angry. Pissed at her for taking off without even a goodbye. *You fucked with her head and her heart. How was she supposed to feel?* "She's not here, Dad. She's back in Los Angeles."

Another coughing spell took his father's breath so his next words were mumbled in a faint whisper Noah had to lean forward to hear. "I know she left suddenly, and I won't pry into what happened between you two, but Noah, you love her. I see it in your eyes, and if you don't make this right, you'll never forgive yourself. I know you too well, son. She is what is important."

Noah clasped his father's hand, not sure if his dad had gone off the deep end or what in his last few days. Love her? He wasn't so sure. Yes, they had amazing chemistry and their lovemaking was off the charts, but love her? The thought scared the shit out of him. The two weeks they'd been together in his house were the best time of his life and since she'd left, the place wasn't the same. Lonely, desolate, and way too quiet for his taste. He'd even started playing some guitar while he was alone to fill the void. Writing lyrics? He couldn't think past his own melancholy thoughts to write anything with a hard beat. Everything that came out on paper seemed sad and rough, the kind of songs made from broken hearts. She hadn't broken his heart too, had she? "I'm not sure if I can fix what I've done. I hurt her, badly."

"Love heals all wounds. She loves you too. I saw it in the way she looked at you."

Had his dad seen something he'd been too blind to see? Had the hole in his chest opened up when she walked out? Did he even want to find out if there was a future there? He'd chased women for so long without any thought to their feelings or what was lacking in his life, he wasn't sure he could see beyond that with Tori.

His mother came to the side of the bed, gently smoothing back the thinning hair on his father's head. The love reflected in her eyes took his breath away. He'd always taken for granted that his parents loved each other, but as his father lay in bed, struggling for his last breaths, his mother was there to hold his hand and ease his passing. She would be by his side until the end, no matter what her own needs were. With a press of her lips to his forehead, she whispered something in his father's ear before moving out the door.

Noah took a moment to take in what he'd just witnessed between his parents. Isn't that what he wanted in the long run? Didn't he want to find the one special person he was meant to be with for the rest of his life or did he want to continue to fuck anything that moved just to avoid complications?

The moment he walked into the house and realized the eerie silence was because she was gone, he'd raced around the house like a madman trying to find her. At that point, he would have given anything for even a hint she'd been there, a hair tie, her scent, a piece of clothing she'd forgotten…anything. The only thing he had to remember her was the smell of her shampoo on his pillow.

With his father's hand pressed to his chest, he said, "I'll give it my best shot."

"Good. I have every faith in you." His father coughed again, bringing his frail chest off the bed before a sip of water held to his mouth finally calmed him enough he could rest against the pillows. "I need to rest now."

Noah put his lips to his dad's forehead and whispered, "I love you, Pop. Hang on just a little longer."

Chapter Twelve

Noah nervously shoved his fingertips through his hair as he paced the conference room where he was to meet with Hilbert, Tori, Blaine, and the attorney for both her and the magazine. He hadn't seen her for over a month, and it felt like forever since he'd touched her, held her, and kissed her. God, he missed her like the devil. Life without Tori had been miserable.

The room was a typical boardroom set up with dark furniture—thickly padded executive chairs surrounding a huge oblong table. A computer console took up the middle of the table and he absently wondered what it was for. Picturing Tori commanding the space took his breath away.

He'd suggested they meet at the magazine's headquarters since it would be easier for Tori and their people. All he wanted was to get this over with and hopefully be talking things through with her on a personal level before the afternoon was over, if she could forgive him for his stupidity. Groveling wasn't part of his repertoire, but he'd do it…for her.

The door opened, giving him his first look at her since she'd left. Her hair hung in waves around her shoulders, looking soft and inviting. Her eyes were clear green, reminding him of the grass growing on his lawn at home. Her lips turned down at the first sight of him as she stopped short and then moved on around the opposite side of the table from him. *Not a good sign.*

"Tori."

"Noah," she replied, grasping the back of the chair in front of her. "I didn't know you'd be here."

He moved closer, but she stepped away, putting the table between them again. "I told them not to tell you. I was afraid you wouldn't show up."

She glanced down at her hands for a moment before squaring her shoulders and looking him in the eye. "I wouldn't have."

Hilbert, Blaine, and the magazine's attorney came in a second later. "Please, everyone, take a seat and we'll get started," Hilbert said, directing things as Noah hoped he would. Hilbert pulled out some papers from the folder he'd set on the tabletop. "You all are aware of the suit pending against the magazine and Victoria Richmond for slander and defamation of character?"

"That's bullshit!" Blaine jumped to his feet, slamming his hand on the table. "We never printed anything that wasn't true, and we did not slander Mr. King's name."

"Mr. Reese, please sit down and shut your mouth," their attorney said as he turned toward Hilbert. "Yes, we are aware of the suit."

Tori's face was white as the blouse she wore. "Mr. Blue, can I say something? I need to clear the air here."

He leaned toward her, whispering in her ear and she turned and said something back. Mr. Blue nodded as Tori turned back toward Noah and Hilbert.

"I wrote the article, but not every word in it."

Blaine's face turned purple. "Shut up, Tori."

She shot a glance at Blaine and said, "You can't tell me what to do anymore, Blaine. I don't work for you, so can it. I want to clear up this misconception before it goes any further."

She doesn't work for Rock Band News anymore?

When her gaze fixed on Noah, he could see something there he didn't want to hope for. Maybe she still cared, even a little. Hope was all he had left.

"The information the guys from Iron Rogue gave me was in the article, yes, but not entirely. Blaine embellished on the truth, stretching every word in there until it screamed, to sell magazines. He's the one who made up the headline that Noah had spilled the secrets to the lyrics of Dare to Love. Noah never told me what those lyrics meant and by the time I was done, I respected his privacy."

"Only because he was giving you orgasms!"

Tori gasped, embarrassment flushed her cheeks red. Surely Blaine didn't know the two of them had been sleeping together. It was only a guess, right?

"I knew it!" He pointed at Noah, his eyes turning fierce and dangerous. "You were fucking her like every other woman you've come across, and she fell for it hook, line, and sinker." He faced Tori, blasting her with his anger. "You are such a stupid bitch. He's a rock star. He doesn't give a shit about you or anything you stand for. He can have any woman he wants. Do you really think he wants you?"

During his tirade, Noah had slowly come to his feet, taking a few steps toward Blaine, but when he verbally attacked Tori, Noah was finished listening. He pulled back his fist and punched Blaine in the mouth. "You will *not* talk to her like that."

Hilbert grabbed Noah's arm, holding him back from doing further damage. "Noah, this is not the way to handle this."

"You tell me what is because I want his fucking job. I want him ruined." The anger he felt toward the man, held no bounds. He would see Blaine Reese in the depths of hell.

Hilbert guided him back to his seat, taking the one next to him. "Ms. Richmond, the suit against you has been dropped by Mr. King and Iron Rogue. Mr. King doesn't believe you maliciously did anything to hurt him or the band by your article and with what you've told us, we understand Mr. Reese took it upon himself to fabricate information under your name."

Tori took a deep breath, exhaling on a sigh. When she raised her gaze to his, the look of hurt in her eyes almost did him in. Relief finally washed it away a moment later.

"I'm sorry I didn't trust you, Tori."

"Water under the bridge, Noah. I've moved on."

"We need to talk."

She shook her head and rose to her feet.

She's leaving? Oh hell, no! He got to his feet to follow her. Explanations were in order and he had to tell her he loved her. "Tori, wait, please?"

"Noah, we aren't finished," Hilbert said, trying to forestall his departure.

"You can handle it from here. The suit stands against Rock Band News and Blaine Reese." By the time he turned around, she was gone.

* * * *

"Damn it! Why did he have to be there? I would have been much better off if he hadn't shown up." God, he looked gorgeous in those low-slung jeans, button-down white shirt rolled up to his elbows to show off the tattoos on his forearms, and the hair. She wanted to run her fingers through it and feel it against her palms. She's always loved his hair and how it would curtain them when they made love.

His eyes had held something she didn't want to name, but it made her heart thump just the same. His lips lifted in a small smile when she'd come into the room, making him look like he was almost happy to see her. *What a crock of shit. He doesn't care about me, just like Blaine said. I'm another notch on his belt, nothing more.*

Tori hit the unlock button for her car as she stepped near the door.

"Tori!"

She closed her eyes, hoping he would just go away. Seeing him hurt. Hearing her name on his lips tortured her soul until she felt like crying, and she didn't want to do that anymore. Enough was enough.

The door handle in her hand, she pulled open the door only to have it shut abruptly.

"Tori, please. I came all this way."

Fury pushed all thoughts of anything nice about the guy from her head and her heart. "*You* came all this way," she whispered through clenched teeth. When she turned to face him, he took a step back. "I don't give a flying fuck whether you flew to the moon, Noah. I told you, I'm done. I have a new job and a life without you in it, so leave me the hell alone. I don't want you. I don't need you, and I certainly don't give a shit what you want."

His fingers brushed her arm, and she couldn't help but shudder at his touch, not in revulsion like she'd hoped, but with a need to feel his hand stroking her flesh and touching her like he had before—like he cared.

"I know you're mad, baby. You have every right to be furious at me. I fucked up. I lost your trust. I hurt you more than any woman deserves to be hurt. I get that. I really do." He pushed her hair off her shoulder, slipping it behind her ear. Goosebumps chased his touch across her shoulder.

"Don't," she breathed, unable to put much conviction behind her words now with her body reacting to him like it was. "I'm done being hurt by you, Noah. Do you hear me? I'm done." She pulled open the car door, slamming it before he could say another word. The engine roared and the tires spun as she gunned it out of the parking garage, leaving him standing in the empty space.

Tears clouded her vision during her race across town to reach the sanctity of her apartment. *Only a few minutes. Only a few minutes and I can cry until my throat is raw.*

The moment she reached for the door, her hands shook as she tried desperately to insert the key in the lock of her apartment for the third time. "Damn it!" A choking sob broke from her lips, her forehead pressed to the door. "Why can't he just leave me alone?" She slid down the door, turning so the back of her head rested against the panel.

"Because he loves you."

Her bag clutched to her chest, her eyes flew open and a startled breath escaped her mouth.

Noah stood at the open elevator doors a few feet away, his gaze pleading for her to understand, and yes, filled with love.

His boots echoed a soft clicking sound on the tile floor as he moved closer. When he crouched down beside her, he ran a finger down her wet cheek before erasing the tears with his thumb. "I don't want you to ever cry because of me again," he whispered, leaning in to place a kiss to her forehead.

He took her keys from her hand and unlocked the door. Sweeping an arm behind her back and one under her knees, he lifted her high against his body and walked inside her apartment. The door shut with a kick of his foot.

With her still in his arms, he sat down on the couch and pulled her in so she rested against his chest. Unable to think clearly being this close to him, she settled in and enjoyed being there for as long as it took to get her head on straight. He shouldn't be there. How did he find her? Why was he there?

Her head popped up, and she stared right into his intense eyes. "Wait. You love me?"

Noah brushed his lips against her, forcing a tortured groan from her mouth. God, she missed him. His hand burrowed into the hair at the nape of her neck, holding her head in place, and he deepened the kiss with a brush of his tongue.

Answers. She needed answers.

"Tell me," she whispered, breaking the onslaught of his mouth.

"I love you, Tori."

She searched his eyes for the truth, finding only love reflected in them.

"I didn't realize how much you meant to me until you were gone. I can't eat. I can't sleep, and God knows, I can't write lyrics for shit."

She laughed a hiccupping sob that made her nose run.

A tissue appeared in her hand from the box next to him on the couch.

"You don't have to say it back if you aren't feeling it, but rest assured, I plan on kidnapping you, holding you at my house, and making love to you until you can't hold back the words." He pushed a piece of her hair behind her ear. "I love you more than anything in this world, and I want you in my life."

His gaze was sincere as he held her face in his hands, his thumbs brushing against her jawline.

Her heart hammered in her chest, thumping so loudly, she thought for sure he could hear it. "I love you too. I've been miserable since I came home. Nothing has been the same here. My life, my work…everything. I need you, Noah. I need you to love me and be my everything."

He lifted her and then turned her so she was straddling his hips, her arms around his broad shoulders, and her hair falling over them like a curtain as she leaned in and brought their mouths together. The slow tongue-stroking kiss seemed to go on forever yet not long enough. A growl escaped him and then he took and took from her mouth—lips crashing together, tongues lashing, and desire soaring.

His lips left hers to scorch a path across her cheek to the spot below her ear that always made her toes curl. A soft nip to the skin forced a shudder through her before he cut a path across her shoulder, pushing her shirt out of his way as he went.

Her head fell back on her shoulders, giving him full access to whatever he wanted and she could tell he planned to take his fill.

Her shirt and bra fell away, leaving her bare to his gaze. "God, you are so beautiful."

He ran his tongue over the tip of her breast and then blew cool air over it, pulling the nub into a tight, aching point. "Noah, please." Her body hummed with desire and the need to touch him.

Her hands shook as she skimmed her palms over his pecs, and then the white buttons down his shirt were no match for her seeking fingers. The smattering of dark chest hair tickled her palms with each pass over his impressive pecs. His body was made for admiring, every valley and every plane seemed made for her touch.

His eyes were hooded as a groan escaped his lips. "You're going to kill me."

"What a way to die," she whispered, bringing her mouth to the pulse beating wildly at the base of his neck. She planned to drive him out of his mind with every lick and nip of his flesh.

He pulled her up so they were nose to nose, his mouth hovering over hers. "I love you so much."

"I love you too."

"I need to feel you beneath me," he breathed against her lips. "I've missed you."

A small smile lifted the corners of his mouth as she shimmied off his lap and took his hand to lead him into her bedroom. Later, she would bring him into her world. Tonight, they needed to reconnect.

Large than life, he commanded her small space. Standing next to her bed, she pushed the shirt off his shoulders, letting it fall at their feet. Her fingers worked the button of his jeans, quickly divesting him of the denim, leaving him naked and fully aroused.

"My, my. Someone is very, hard." Her palm glided over the silky skin of his arousal, tracing the bulging vein until she encircled his length. "Do you want me?"

"You have no fucking idea how badly I want you."

Wetness already coated her panties from nothing more than his kisses, she couldn't wait to feel his tongue on her most intimate parts again.

His fingers skimmed over her bare shoulder, sliding down until it encircled the peak of her breast, lifting the weight in his palm before he wrapped his mouth around it and sucked. She came up on her toes as he ran his tongue over the nipple, flicking it until she wanted to scream. "Noah, please."

He lifted his head, his eyes glazed with a fiery passion she hadn't seen before. "Oh, baby. We've got all night, and I plan to make you come over and over before I take my fill of your gorgeous body."

Walking her back a couple of steps, he reached around to unzip the back of her skirt and draw it along with her silky panties down over her hips.

"You looked so prim and proper today in that conference room. I wanted nothing more than to lay you out on the table and fuck you until everyone in the entire office heard you scream my name."

"Oh, God," she whispered, wanting to feel him so badly she ached with it.

He gently laid her back on the bed, following her down until his chest brushed hers and then captured her lips in a soul-searing kiss. As he worked his way down her body, stopping to lick and suck each nipple in turn until they stood up in aching points, he moved down her abdomen until he hovered right above her sex.

A small push to his shoulders drew a laugh from his mouth. "I know what I'm doing, sweetheart, and I know what you want, but you'll get it when I'm ready to give it to you."

Sitting back on his haunches, he brought her foot to his lips, licking the skin on the inside of her ankle as he shot her a smoldering look from between her legs. His tongue cut a path from there up the inside of her leg until he reached her knee where he licked and sucked the back and sides until she was squirming. The warm chuckle against her flesh made goose bumps chase each other to her center. He tortured the other leg the same way until she felt like she would crawl out of her skin, she wanted him so badly.

Her thighs quivered as his mouth drew closer. A whimper escaped her lips while she fisted the bed covers in her hands. She bit her bottom lip, trying desperately to force down her need.

The first swipe of his tongue over her swollen clit had her hips coming off the bed. "Ah, God!"

"We are just getting started, baby." His hand pressed her hips back down, taking his fill of her like a starving man. "Your scent is intoxicating." He pressed his nose to the crease between her thigh and her belly, inhaling her. "Even here, it lingers."

Two fingers pressed deep into her channel, scraping in a rasping, erotic path in and out until she wanted to scream.

The brush of his whiskered chin and cheek against her inner thigh as he kissed her had her whimpering in need, wishing to God he would apply a little pressure where she needed it the most. He flattened his tongue, drinking her in until she couldn't hold back any longer, screaming with her orgasm. "Noah!"

"I'm sorry, love. I can't wait to be inside you," he whispered, desperation clear in his voice. He crawled back up her body, capturing her mouth with his as if he would die without a taste of her.

"Now. Please, Noah."

With her legs around his hips, he pushed the head of his cock into her, groaning heavily. "I've missed you, so much. You are my world, Tori." He brushed his lips against hers, nipping at her mouth until she moaned out her need.

The feel of him, the weight, the taste, the way he moved…it would never be enough no matter if they had the rest of their lives.

Twenty minutes later, after two more orgasms and Noah coming inside her, she lay with her head on his chest playing with the swirl of hair under her palms. His heart had slowed to a steady rhythm, one she knew well, as his fingers ran a soft pattern over her upper arm with his fingers.

"How is your dad?"

"Not well. I'm not sure how long he has left. He's pretty much bedridden now and very sickly looking."

"I'm sorry," she whispered, grabbing the sheet to her chest as she sat up. "You need to go home and be with him, Noah. I'm sure he wants you by his side."

Noah touched her shoulder, drawing her back down to his chest. "Baby, he's the one who told me to come and find you. He saw the love between us long before we did, I think. He wants me to bring you home with me."

Home? Back to Iowa? My life is here, in Los Angeles. My job is here. She bit her lip to hold back the sobs.

"What's wrong?" he asked, propping himself up against the headboard. "You're awfully quiet."

She shook her head, not wanting to mess up their time together. Sadness brought the happiness she'd felt having him there to a screeching halt. How would they ever make a relationship work when they were so far apart? "Nothing. Just thinking."

"You're thinking too much. We love each other. Whatever problem arises, we'll deal with together."

Pressing a kiss to his chest, she rose to the side of the bed and grabbed her clothes. "There are obstacles. Things I'm not sure we can get over"

"Nothing is too big, Tori." He touched her arm, but she shied away, pulling her arm from his reach.

A tear slipped down her cheek the moment she disappeared behind the bathroom door. She needed a minute to compose herself and wash the smell of sex off her body. *I should never have let him touch me. I should have shut the door on this whole thing before we got to this point. Now, it's going to be hell walking away again.*

His voice came from just the other side. "Don't shut me out, Tori."

"I can't do this right now, Noah. Go, please."

"This isn't over." A heavy sigh reached her ears moments before she heard the door to her bedroom close.

The choking sob that ripped from her sounded like her world had ended. Her butt hit the cold tile of the bathroom floor as she curled up in a ball and cried until her throat was raw.

Chapter Thirteen

A soft knock on her bathroom door brought Tori's head up. *Please don't let it be Noah. I can't handle him right now.*

"Tori, honey, open the door." It was Bella.

The lock twisted slowly in her fingers until Bella managed to open it and slide inside.

"Lord, look at you," she said, slipping to the floor beside Tori and pulling her into her embrace. "You are a mess, girl."

Giving Bella a watery smile, she couldn't hold back the tears as they rolled down her cheeks again. "I can't do this again, Bell. My heart can't handle it," she whispered.

"Do what, sweetie?"

"Walk away from him. I just can't."

Bella pushed the hair from Tori's eyes before she grabbed a corner of the sheet and wiped her face. "Why would you do that, Tori? You love him, and I'm pretty sure he loves you."

"But my career is here. My life…"

The look in Bella's eyes took Tori back a second. Fury in her friend's gaze made her feel small and really, *really* stupid.

"Are you fucking crazy or what?"

"I don't know what you mean."

Bella climbed to her feet to pace the bathroom with her hands fisted at her sides. "You have a man who is madly in love with you and you're going to give up the best thing in your life for a job? A job, Tori? Really? Is your career so important to you that you will walk away from happiness?" Bella sat down on the floor beside her again, her legs crossed and her head back against the door. "Do you know what I would give to have the love of a good man?"

Guilt played hell with her heart. She knew Noah loved her, he'd said as much, and she didn't think he would say those words lightly. Her heart belonged to him, everything that she was fit in the palm of his hand because she couldn't think beyond being with him and here she was over thinking again. She loved him, damn it, so why was she sitting here on the floor of her bathroom trying to push him away? To love someone meant becoming one with them and putting aside your own needs and wants to the betterment of who you are together, not separate. "You're right, Bell. He's everything to me and I'm nothing without him. If my job won't work with me in order for us to be together, then I'll find something else." The corner of the sheet became her tissue as she wiped her face and got to her feet. "I need to find him."

"I don't think you'll have to look far."

Tori combed her hair out and pulled it back into a ponytail, before scrubbing her face until it glowed. "Why not?"

"He's sitting on your couch."

Her gaze meant Bella's in the mirror and she saw the love of a good friend in her gaze.

One shoulder lifted in a half shrug. "Sorry. I came over to check on you after your mediation and found him pacing your apartment." Bella leaned in and kissed her on the cheek. "He's hot, by the way, and he looked so broken, I had to help."

Tori grabbed her friend in a hug as she whispered, "Thank you for the kick in the butt."

When they parted, Bella smiled. "You're welcome." Her gaze softened as it ran over Tori's face. "Be happy, sweetie. You deserve it more than anyone I know." Bella slipped out with a soft click of the door.

Tori went into her bedroom and threw on a pair of shorts and a tank top, needing clothes between them to keep things as unsexy as possible.

When she opened the door, Noah turned to face her, his eyes sad, his hair, all that gorgeous hair, down around his shoulders, his chest bare, and nothing on but his jeans.

"Hey."

Scared to hope they could work things out, she took a few tentative steps in his direction. "Hey."

He crossed the expanse between them, sweeping his fingers into her hair at the base of her neck and bracketing her face with his palms. "I love you."

Her heart opened to accept what he said. "I love you, too." The itching of threatening tears made her blink several times. "I'm sorry." With her hands wrapped around his wrists, she looked up into his dark eyes, reading every bit of love in them she'd hoped for her entire life. "I'm scared, Noah. I'm terrified love isn't enough with my career, the band, the touring, and everything. I don't want to get to the point where we hate each other."

"Baby, I'm scared too. I've never felt like this with anyone before, but it's a good scared. It's an excited scared. I can't promise we'll never fight. Lord knows we're both stubborn and a little pigheaded."

A watery laugh escaped her lips as he pressed a kiss to her forehead.

"But we have love and that means everything."

The brush of his lips against hers had her moaning into his mouth as their tongues tangled, searching for that connection they both knew they couldn't deny. Their hearts beat as one, the same rhythm, each looking for the one person they were meant to be with for the rest of their lives. They'd finally found heaven.

"Promise me one thing."

"Anything."

"You'll never go to bed angry with me."

She laughed as she pulled his head back in for another kiss and whispered against his lips, "I promise never to go to bed angry with you. Now, kiss me like you mean it."

A soft growl came from his mouth as he devoured her from the corners of her lips to her upper lip before he took what he wanted in a kiss that left no room for doubt as to his feelings for her.

Following her down on the couch, he hovered over her, nipping at her flesh, feasting on her until she whimpered beneath him. "More."

The thin straps of her tank top were no match for his seeking mouth. The soft skim over her skin had goosebumps chasing every move he made. Her nipples pebbled, aching for him to touch them, kiss them, suck them—something. Once he'd bared them to his gaze, he slipped his tongue over the peaks before blowing on them, leaving a cool sensation. The ache intensified to something beyond her imagination.

Wetness coated her panties, her need pushing to excruciatingly painful. "God, please Noah. I need you."

Desire and need turned his gaze scorching, the flame burning for only her as he grasped her shorts and slid them down her hips, taking her panties with them. "I can smell your desire, kitten. You are gorgeous." He positioned himself between her parted thighs, brushing the inside of her legs with his lips. The slow glide of his mouth, closer and closer to her clit, had her whimpering and grasping at his shoulders. "I know what you need. Relax and let me love you."

The moment his tongue slipped over her clit, her hips came off the couch. Noises she didn't know she could make, sprang from her lips as he continued to feast on her. His tongue slid up one side, then the other, before he grasped her clit between his lips and sucked.

"OhGodohGodohGod!"

Her breath left her lungs in a rush, and her climax crashed over her like waves on the shore, the minute he reached up and pinched her left nipple between his finger and his thumb.

He continued to lick her until her heart slowed and breathing returned to close to normal.

"Oh, baby. You are so beautiful when you come," he said, taking her lips in a bruising kiss. "God, I need to be inside you." He pushed his jeans down his thighs, wiggling until he had them off and on the floor beside the couch.

"Now, Noah. Please, now," she begged, feeling empty without his cock inside her.

"Condom."

Her gaze locked on his. "I'm clean and I haven't been with anyone but you in over two years."

"Two years? Holy shit." He leaned in and kissed her. "I'm not worried about you, baby, so much as me. I haven't had sex with anyone without a condom in years, but I don't want to risk your health. I was tested about a year ago, but let me get it run one more time and then we can go bare." He drove his tongue into her mouth, taking and taking until she could barely breathe without him there. "I can't wait to feel every hot inch of you as I push inside you without anything between us. God, that makes me ache for you beyond what I can handle right now."

He reached for his pants, retrieving a condom from his wallet and rolling it down his length. The stretch of her body, as it accommodated his cock, had her whimpering her desire as she said, "Yes. God yes." She clawed at his back with her nails, sure she was leaving marks on his magnificent flesh. Her need tore at her insides as he began his slow glide, bringing her up and up until she couldn't hold back her cries. Her climax exploded through her, tearing his name from her mouth on a desperate scream.

He pressed his forehead to hers as he continued his assault on her senses, then pressing kisses to her cheeks, her eyelids, her mouth, and her ear. "God, I love you so much. You're my world."

"Love me, Noah. Please, love me."

Shoving both hands under her ass, he brought her hips up, changing the angle of his penetration until they were both breathing hard and holding nothing back.

He shouted with his orgasm at the same time she panted his name over and over, loving every minute of his possessive coupling.

A laugh escaped his lips as he pushed her hair back off her forehead. "I guess we both need a shower now."

"Only if you'll join me and then we can talk." A frown drew his eyebrows down, but she took her finger and smoothed it away. "Nothing bad. We have plans to make if we are going to figure out how this is going to work."

The lift of his lips in his signature crooked grin made her heart do a little flip in her chest.

Noah King loved her!

* * * *

Noah listened as Tori paced behind the couch, her phone pressed to her ear. This whole relationship thing and compromising between what he wanted and needed and her was new to him. He'd do it though. She was his world.

"Yes, I know I just started there, Abe, but this is something I have to do. Are you willing to work with me on a remote basis for my assignments? I can still come to Los Angeles and spend a week every month or so." She caught his gaze, and he gave her an affirmative nod. He'd do anything for her and hoped she knew that. If it meant working their touring around her schedule, then so be it. The smile she gave him, lit up the room. He had enough money that if she didn't want to work, she didn't have to, but somehow he figured that might be hard for her to accept.

"Good. I'll see you in the morning then, and we can discuss the details." She stopped pacing and blew him a kiss. "Perfect. Thank you."

He and Tori would go back to Iowa in a few weeks after making arrangements with Abe on her job. They could stay in Los Angeles until right before Iron Rogue went back on tour. The magazine would hopefully be more than willing to let her work remotely, and it gave her inside access to the up and coming bands who opened for Iron Rogue. Perfect for the roving reporter they wanted, plus exclusive content.

She leaned over the back of the couch, and he turned to capture her lips in a soul-stealing kiss. "I love you."

"Love you, too."

"So, he's okay with you working remotely and coming in for a week?"

"Seems to be," she said, coming around the couch to sit down beside him. "He's a great guy, Noah. I'm sure everything will be okay. I have an appointment with him in the morning, which is fine since I have to work in the office tomorrow anyway, and we can go over the details."

"I want to be there."

Her eyes rolled before focusing on his again. "I'm a big girl. I can handle this." She climbed over his lap, straddling his hips. "Now, kiss me before I explode from lack of kisses."

"Needy wench."

"When it comes to you, definitely."

She leaned in for a kiss, but he stopped her with his finger pressed against her lips. Her frown told him she didn't understand. This was important and he wanted her complete attention.

"Something wrong?"

"Tori, I want you to write an article about the band."

A small grin lifted her lips. "I already did."

He had to make her understand. "No, I want you to rewrite the one you already wrote with one change."

She tipped her head to the side as she focused on his face. This was important and something he wanted to do for her.

"What change?"

"I'm going to give you the scoop on the lyrics of Dare to Love."

Her mouth dropped open as she stared at his face. "You aren't serious."

"Definitely serious."

"But you said you would never tell." She sat back and framed his face with her hands, pressing her fingers into his jawline.

"I know, but this is important for you and for me. Now that I have you, keeping the secret to those lyrics doesn't mean anything."

"I don't understand."

"Those lyrics were for you," he whispered, pressing a kiss to her lips.

Her eyes widened and stared straight into his.

He took a piece of her hair, rubbing it between his thumb and finger. The softness always amazed him, leaving him with the need to touch her. He pressed his palm into the crook of her neck, cupping it right below her ear as he looked into her eyes. "I wrote those with the woman I searched for in mind. The woman I wanted to find to spend my life with. It was a young man's wants and desires to discover his forever love. You are my forever love, the last words of that song."

"God, Noah," she whispered, a tear slipping down her cheek.

Her lips pressed against his, making him realize he too had some suspicious wetness on his cheeks. "You are my everything, Tori. I don't ever want to lose you again. I couldn't handle it."

"I love you so much it hurts."

A smile spread across his face. "Hurts good, I hope."

Her voice dropped to a sexy little purr. "Better than good. Fantastic." Her hand reached inside his shirt, pressing against where his heart lies. "This is it, you know. Dare to Love only me."

"Only you."

Epilogue

Rain did a little pitter-patter on the umbrella over their heads as they stood near the gaping hole that would be his father's final resting place. His father had passed in his sleep two days ago, his mother lying by his side and his children around his bed.

The preacher's voice droned on and on, a monotone sermon he didn't hear much of. The only thing he could focus on was Tori's warm palm in his, grounding him and helping him make it through the day. He loved her more every day.

"You okay?" she asked softly, peeking up at him through her lashes, her eyes sad and searching.

"Yeah."

"I love you."

"I love you, too." He pressed a kiss to the back of her hand. "Thanks for being here."

"Always."

The moment they lowered his father's casket, he looked across the expanse of the cemetery. It was over. The pain his father had endured the last few months, the need to make everything right before he could rest, and the happiness in his dad's eyes the day he'd brought Tori back with him, it all made sense now. His father still controlled every aspect of his life until the day he'd passed.

"Let's go home," Tori said, turning toward the waiting cars.

They still had to greet the mourners at his parents' place and do all of that. It wasn't something he was looking forward to, but as long as Tori was by his side, he could handle anything.

Several hours later, he opened the door to his house, drawing Tori inside as he shut the world out.

A sigh escaped his lips as he took her hand and led her to the couch, taking her down onto the cushion with him.

"You did great today."

He drew her in for a kiss, pressing his lips to hers unhurried, but thorough. "How did I get so lucky to have fallen in love with you?"

"Fate."

"Hmm. Yeah, I think so."

"Do you want something to drink?" she asked, climbing to her feet.

He pulled her back down beside him. "No, I want you."

"Sounds good to me."

"Forever," he said, slipping his hands into her hair and holding her face in his palms. "I know this probably isn't the best timing, but I need to make something good out of today."

"What are you saying, Noah?"

"Marry me."

"Marry you?"

"Yes. Say you will, at least. Two weeks from now. A month from now. A year from now. I don't care, just say you'll be my wife."

She searched his eyes for what seemed like forever, until he thought he'd go crazy waiting for her to answer.

"Are you sure?" she whispered.

"I've never been more sure of anything in my life." He dug into his pants pocket, pulling out the ring box he'd been carrying around for several weeks. "Say yes, kitten."

"Yes. More than anything, yes!"

The End

About the Author

Sandy Sullivan is a romance author, who, when not writing, spends her time with her husband Shaun on their farm in middle Tennessee. She loves to ride her horses, play with their dogs and relax on the porch, enjoying the rolling hills of her home south of Nashville. Country music is a passion of hers and she loves to listen to it while she writes, although when she writes sex scenes, it has to be completely quiet.

She is an avid reader of romance novels and enjoys reading Nora Roberts, Jude Deveraux and Susan Wiggs. Finding new authors and delving into something different helps feed the need for literature. A registered nurse by education, she loves to help people and spread the enjoyment of romance to those around her with her novels. She loves cowboys so you'll find many of her novels have sexy men in tight jeans and cowboy boots. This newest passion includes rock stars who are moody, but need to find the woman of their dreams too.

www.romancestorytime.com